THE
PRESIDENT'S
CADDY

The President's Caddy

A Golf Story

Tony Rosa

 Jackpot PRESS

The President's Caddy
Copyright © 2014 by Anthony J. Rosa

Purchase through booksellers or by contacting:
JackpotPress@gmail.com

This is a work of fiction. All of the characters, names, incidents, places, organizations, and dialogue in this golf story are either the products of the author's imagination or are used fictitiously.

The character Ernie Banks and his career statistics in baseball are included in this story as a tribute. Any and all dialogue, mannerisms, incidents associated with Mr. Banks in this golf story are the product of the author's imagination and are used fictitiously.

ISBN-13: 978-0-9828225-0-0
ISBN-10: 0982822502

THE
PRESIDENT'S
CADDY

We wish to assert our existence, like dogs peeing on fire hydrants. We put on display our framed photographs, our parchment diplomas, our silver-plated cups; we monogram our linen, we carve our names on trees, we scrawl them on washroom walls. It's all the same impulse. What do we hope from it? Applause, envy, respect? Or simply attention, of any kind we can get?

-Margaret Atwood, *The Blind Assassin*

1

I sat there on the curb, forearms draped over knees, waiting for a ride home and wondering why I had bothered with any of it. Prickly heat stored from a day in the sun radiated from the gray slab. I rattled a couple of dusty pebbles in one hand then lobbed them in the air like a pair of dice. An ant hiked across the pavement into my shadow. Hoisted on its back was a salvaged crumb from a littered last bite of a hot dog bun. The load was twice the ant's size and weight. The rugged terrain of the asphalt gave it fits of stops and starts. Although the course it traveled was anything but straight, the ant finally found a familiar crack in the roadway and then disappeared.

Futile—that's the word I was looking for. That's what I was feeling. And yeah, I knew what the word meant. I looked it up. I could've used others like useless, pointless, or wasted. Any of those would've done just fine. But I settled on futile.

Once you find out how I arrived at this spot, you'll understand.

Trying to follow a few simple rules of being a caddy had turned out to be a total disaster. If the whole ordeal was some kind of test, I had probably made somewhere around a D-minus. If you had asked me when the day began, I would've said there was no way I could sink so low. But any confidence, enthusiasm, or excitement I had at the start had been slowly drained like a busted engine leaking oil.

As I sat there waiting for my ride, I tried to recall a bright spot. I had plenty of time to think. The only thing I could come up with was that I had at least followed one rule of being a caddy; I had made it to the golf course on time. But the more I thought about it, my uncle had more to do with that accomplishment than I did.

And before anyone gets to thinking that flubbing up a few caddy rules shouldn't get a person feeling so low, there's more to it. Much more. Not to mention a mistake, an error, a blunder, a goof, so monumental, so boneheaded, so colossal, it would probably be retold around the world for months and years to come. The knucklehead move of the century was noteworthy enough for me to give it a name.

The Big Goof.

So, add humiliation and embarrassment to the list.

A Saturday filled with futility and shame. Sat-On-A-Turd-Day was more like it. The way things had gone, it wouldn't have surprised me if I had sat down in something sticky. I rocked forward and glanced behind me. The cracked slab was blank. To make sure, I rose and took a halfhearted swat at the seat of my pants.

A waft of burnt grease charcoal smoke reached my nose. A grill behind a nearby corporate tent was working overtime. Thumping live music drummed my ears.

Once on my feet, I had a better view down the street. I placed cupped hands to the visor bill as if looking through binoculars. It added very little improvement in my ability to see further. I looked over the hoods of parked cars, past the uniformed guard at the entrance, and down the tree-lined cobblestone sidewalk. As if the act of looking itself, not to mention the extra shading of the sun, would bring the station wagon any faster.

It seemed like I was always waiting for a ride home; after school, after baseball practice, after work. It felt like everyone else left the parking lot before me. It was always me stranded on a deserted island. And yeah, that's right, I had had a job over the previous summer. I could get my driver's license under one condition; I could pay for the insurance. I turned sixteen last week. Needless to say, I was still short a driver's license.

I sank back to the curb and continued the wait. It was always the same lonely feeling.

Matthew seemed to never wait. Even today, he wasn't bothered with it. After the round, he was whisked away to cozy confines by a corporate bigwig where he was to fill his belly with all the ice cream floats he could handle. It seemed Matthew was always falling into good fortune. All day he had been the darling of the crowd with his charm and cuteness. He knew nothing about futile feelings. He had a splendid day. I wished him nothing more than a brain freeze that would cause temporary blindness and a stomachache that would keep him up all night.

And Renee. She never appeared too concerned about waiting either. As I walked to the parking lot, she basically ignored me. "Come and get me when Mom gets here," she said, never really looking in my direction. She was leaning against a tree trunk batting her eyes at some dopey dude. She twisted a looped finger in her necklace while snapping her gum and oozing goofy giggling noises. The dude had to be older than her, probably out of high school. Mister Moustache. I'd never seen him around. He was wearing the visor that Uncle Charlie had given to her.

Sat-On-A-Turd-Day.

Futile.

For some reason I thought about the bare patch in Mrs. Eckleburg's lawn. I've heard the saying that misery loves company. Well maybe, futile loves company too. Trying to make grass grow in that bare spot left me feeling futile. That's probably why I thought of it while waiting for my ride home. Since I have time, I should probably explain.

I must've been about twelve years old when I took on the job of mowing that lawn, close to Matthew's age right now. And he doesn't mow any lawns. Just last week I asked him to help me with the trimming at Mrs. Eckleburg's. But he didn't even consider it. And she lived just next door.

Outside of an occasional allowance, the money Mrs. Eckleburg paid me was the first income I ever earned. It took me about an hour to push the mower over her yard and trim the places the mower couldn't reach. For the most part, I would lump the money with what slid from a birthday card or came my way over the holidays. I landed the job because Mrs. Eckleburg could no longer do the work herself. On the real sweltering days, I dreaded the work myself. Sweat-soaked, exhausted, and stinking of grass clippings, I couldn't wait for the glass of lemonade and the five dollar bill. She always had both of them waiting on the small table on her patio. To me, it signified the end of the job like a blowing steam whistle at the factory.

As for the bare spot, I'm not even sure why I decided to do something about it. Maybe it was because billows of dust would fly every time I pushed the mower over it. Mrs. Eckleburg shook her head and said she didn't have the time or patience to improve the ragged patch between her sidewalk and house. She hinted the need for improvement. Maybe that was enough for me to take it on. For all I knew, it was probably because I had nothing better to do.

"I don't get it," Renee had criticized. "You're doing all this stuff in hopes to grow more grass? That makes no sense. You're the one doing the mowing. You're creating more work for yourself. That's just crazy."

But Renee never understood. I didn't mind the work. I got some satisfaction out of trying something new and keeping the lawn looking nice. Several times I had tried explaining stuff like that to Renee. But I gave up. I'd simply respond with, "It's not crazy." She couldn't lure me into an argument. There was nothing she could say that would change my mind. She couldn't make me angry either. I just handed her a simple reply, "It's not crazy."

Maybe I just liked the compliments that came with a job well done. If Mrs. Eckleburg or anyone else in the neighborhood happened to mention a noticeable improvement, well I figured that would be worth it. And if that didn't happen, well, I figured any noticeable improvement would give me a little self-satisfaction. And if that wasn't the reason, I guess my motivation wasn't all that important to begin with. I can't remember reasons for doing half the stuff I did.

I found half a bag of grass seed in our shed and asked if I could use it. I didn't even bother asking Mrs. Eckleburg for money. I wanted it to be a surprise. Maybe even a miracle. I figured once she noticed the new growth, she'd certainly appreciate the effort. I gathered around the proper tools. A rake. The hose. I dug. I hauled. I watered. I scraped my hands raw. It took me a week to get the dirt out of my fingernails. I kept an eye on that patch waiting for signs of new life. It was probably the first time I realized the importance of being patient. If I could do a little each day, I figured it would eventually add up to a green lawn. But before there were any signs of growth, I started having doubts.

Mrs. Eckleburg had paid little attention to my efforts. And since there wasn't a noticeable improvement in the lawn, she never had a chance to comment on any result. The miracle never happened. Maybe there just wasn't enough sun on that spot. Then again, maybe it was the seeds in that old bag I had found in the shed. Maybe they were no good to begin with. My own family offered some praise. They said it was nice that I had tried to make something out of nothing regardless of the result.

Don't let me get started down the wrong track; this really isn't a gardening story. Could there be a more boring story than one that involved watching grass grow? It's just how I was feeling, sitting on the sidewalk, waiting for my ride home. The lousy day of being a caddy reminded me of the previous failed effort. It reminded me that futile feelings were nothing new.

And I guess that's the main reason why what happened next made such a profound difference. It more than helped me shake those gloomy feelings.

What happened next changed everything.

In some ways, it made me forget about all that had happened. Most notably, it helped me get over the Big Goof.

Trying to compare myself to Chip Swanson was a big mistake. Maybe I aimed too high. Compared to me, his skills and knowledge of the golf course were far superior. The more I thought about it, Chip Swanson was probably a better caddy than almost everyone. His instructions were colorful and delivered with the confidence of a riverboat gambler. That set him apart. I paid the price for opening my mouth at the wrong time, but at least I tried. I had learned one thing. I still had plenty of room for improvement. My caddying skills were still being honed. If nothing else, the comparison to Chip Swanson taught me that much.

And Teresa Bellissima. Could I have been a bigger fool? Come Monday, I will probably be the biggest laughingstock of the tenth grade. Probably the whole school. If I see her in the halls, should I act dumb, like nothing ever happened? Or, should I do my best to avoid her for the next three years? What a disaster. I wondered if she'll ever speak to me again. If she doesn't, no big loss. I had already figured that I couldn't really lose something I never had in the first place.

But what happened next helped me forget about her too.

When it came to Uncle Charlie, I only hoped I hadn't embarrassed him. That would be devastating. He stuck his neck out for me, and I didn't want him to ever regret it. I tried to be careful and cautious. But even that proved to be a mistake. I only hoped Uncle Charlie's reputation was spared.

I was looking for a bright spot in the day, and now I realized I had spent the last four hours in the company of one of baseball's greatest players. Meeting Ernie Banks was a highlight. He made the day fun. And although remembering that as a bright spot, it wasn't the thing that lifted me from the doldrums. It would take more than that.

And the President. Well, he might as well have been just about anybody. I doubt he ever thought much of me from the beginning. I'm not sure he even knew my name. I expended blood and sweat trying to do an extraordinary job. Sure, I made a few mistakes, but the effort was there. Whenever in the future he needed to fill some empty time waiting around on a tee, he could retell dignitaries around the world about the Big Goof. The implausible horror and unspeakable shock and bewilderment would entertain playing partners for years. At least I did that much for him. And yeah, that's right; I'm talking about the President of the United States.

Up to that point, Saturday had felt like a disaster. I sat there waiting for my ride and wondering if I should come up with some kind of excuse to get myself out of caddying the next day. I wanted to abandon all possibilities of a repeat episode. I doubted my own ability. I wanted to never think of being a caddy again. I wanted to hide and forget.

But what happened next changed everything.

Quick as a light switch, what happened changed my outlook.

My spirits were lifted.

After it happened, I felt much better.

I started looking forward to the next day. Sunday. The sun would come out on Sunday.

But I'm getting ahead of myself.

I could tell you what happened next, but it would be meaningless without knowing the whole story. To understand what lifted my spirits, you would have to first know how I arrived at such a low spot.

So, let me get to the beginning of this story. It started with a call from the Secret Service.

2

At times, our house was as frantic and hectic as the floor of the New York Stock Exchange. The hub of chaos was the kitchen. Renee occupied the space between the refrigerator and stove. She was rehearsing her moves as a flag girl in the high school marching band. It was like she was desperate for an audience. She silently counted and marched to the beat of the music playing in her head. She bended, twisted, and flailed her arms that propelled an invisible flag. The stadium might as well have been empty and the lights shut off for all the attention she was paid.

Because carpet was not suitable for jacks, I was on the kitchen floor teaching Megan how to play. She had come home from a classmate's eighth birthday party with the game. "Okay," I said to her, "I'm going for my twosies." I lobbed the rubber ball. It bounced and arced from the shiny linoleum. Before it had a chance to land a second time, I scooped up two of the scattered jacks then caught the ball with the same hand. "See," I said to Megan, showing the gathered pair. "I got my twosies."

In the den, Matthew sat yogi style a few feet from the television screen. He clutched a video game controller and mashed the buttons that maneuvered a spaceship. "Awe, c'mon," he'd occasionally scream while gobbling up points. "I got you." It didn't matter one bit that the virtual aliens remained unresponsive.

"Die! Die!" Every streaking rocket, every slicing laser beam, and every deep-space minefield explosion resonated through the house.

Megan looked at me with a smile. "Now what?"

"I go for threesies." I surveyed the remaining jacks on the floor for a cluster. I tossed the ball in the air again.

"For once," my mom said, hunched over the counter. A lock of hair had fallen in front of her face. It wiggled as she spoke. "I wish you would've told me about the cookies before now." I thought she was beyond the scolding stage. But it appeared her frayed nerves still simmered.

Megan mushroomed her bottom lip. "But I forgot." An appeal of innocent remorse and hopeful mercy. She knew what worked.

My mom flipped a switch on the mixer. Spinning beaters ticked at the glass sides of the bowl. Each plunge into the thick dough strained the tired electric motor. "You should've told me before now," she said loud enough to overtake the whirring.

Renee high stepped and spun near the pile of scattered jacks. "I better not step on one of them." Her invasion was afoot.

"Back off," I sneered. "We were here first."

As the mixer fell silent, my mom said, "I just wish for once I didn't have to slap something together at the last minute." For all I knew, she had been grumbling a list of complaints as the mixer clashed and whirred. "All because someone forgot to tell me."

"It's my turn to lick the beaters," Matthew shouted from the den.

Renee continued marching in place. She was seventeen and thought she controlled everything in the house. Especially the telephone. She was always lingering around the black box and had a habit of being within reach on the first ring. She acted as if the incoming messages were part of her life support system.

The phone rang.

The flag girl routine came to an abrupt halt. Renee snatched the receiver and pressed it to her ear. She sagged. Along with the nosedive of enthusiasm, she propped the back of her hand on a swung-out hip. "It's for you," she said, motioning in my direction. "Don't take too long," She dangled the handset by the coiled cord. "I'm expecting a call."

Phone calls didn't mean as much to me. And as for Renee's time limit instructions, I stopped paying attention to them when I was about six years old. It seemed she was always ordering me around and dumping steaming bowls of grief atop my head. In her eyes, I could do nothing right. She was an expert at all things. She was an expert at being an expert. To me, that was useless. "You shouldn't wear that shirt," she'd hurl at me. "It's ugly and out-of-style." I often took the bait. "Who cares?" I would respond. "I like it. Other people like it. They get it." She would then fire back with something like, "Well, that just means you don't know anything. And if anyone else likes something you're wearing, that just means they're dumb as you."

I grabbed the phone and placed a hand over the mouthpiece. "Who is it?"

"I don't know," Renee rolled her eyes. "Don't take long."

In no hurry to solve the mystery, I glanced toward the kitchen counter.

"I wanted to make chocolate chip cookies," Megan said, sidling up to my mom and looking into the bowl. "I told the teacher I would bring chocolate chip cookies."

"We're out of chocolate chips."

Thinking it was a friend from school, I used a highbrow voice. "Chell-O".

Matthew yelled from the den. "It's my turn to lick the beaters." He never took his eyes from the glowing screen.

A deep, serious-sounding monotone voice came over the line. "Is this Samuel Gaetano Parma?"

I hesitated then spit out a careful, "Yes."

Megan stomped lightly on the floor. "Can't we go to the store and get chocolate chips?"

On the phone the serious voice rattled off some formal introduction about how they were from some security company and was I planning on being a caddy in a few weeks and how they were preparing some kind of list and then asked me when my birthday was. In a sense, I thought maybe it was the kind of phone call I would get if my name had been drawn out of a barrel to win a grand prize sweepstakes. But the voice on the other end didn't quite match up with such exciting news.

"Look at the clock," my mom pointed a dough-covered finger. "There's no time to go to the store for chocolate chips. That's why you should've told me before now."

I spit out a month, day, and year, and then said, "What's this for again?"

Matthew yelled, "Nobody better be licking the beaters."

"We got your name from the list of people working the Capital City Golf Tournament with close access to the President. This is just routine. For a clearance report prior to his arrival."

Megan whined, "Can I go and ask Mrs. Eckleburg if we can borrow some chocolate chips?"

"But he isn't the *real* President."

"Pardon me, son?"

"I don't think so—" My mom shook her head. "We've been borrowing too many things from Mrs. Eckleburg lately."

"I mean he's not the President anymore," I stammered, feeling confused and intimidated by the inquiry. "It's not like he's doing the job now."

"Son, due to the sensitive diplomatic nature and perpetual ambassadorial status bestowed upon former Presidents, the Secret Service provides lifetime protection. That makes his ongoing safekeeping our responsibility. Young people should have more respect for the office. Once you're President of the United States, you will always be President of the United States; for the rest of your life and beyond. Now, I need to verify your Social Security number."

I didn't mean to sound like a knucklehead, but I guess that's what the voice thought of me. A disrespectable wisenheimer. My heart began to pound.

Renee was looking at the ceiling. "I'm waiting for a phone call." She twitched her head with each word.

I shot back a glare.

The voice got louder and the words came faster. "Do you know your Social Security number?"

Megan continued. "But I wanted chocolate chips."

"I guess not." I placed my hand over the mouthpiece. "Mom." I pointed the receiver in her direction.

She got the message. "I don't want to hear anymore about chocolate chips," she said. "You'll take what we're making." She glanced into the den. "Turn that down," she said to Matthew, dusting her hands on the apron. She grabbed the phone from me. "Hello."

It was a relief at this point to jump out of the hot seat. Some things were better off left to adults.

With a calm demeanor, my mom listened and asked a few questions. She seemed appeased with answers. "Yes," she said, "I have numbers for both of them if you'll just give me a minute." She left the phone on the counter. Within a few minutes she returned with a couple of blue cards she had dug from a fire-proof metal box retrieved from the top shelf of her bedroom closet. Don't ask me how I knew about the metal box. "This is for Sam," she said, reading off a string of numbers.

"You're so lucky," Renee said.

"Me?" I tried not to get sucked into her trap. "What're you talking about?"

"I wish I got to be a caddy."

"How did you even know what this was about?" Her control of the phone included an ability to hear voices on the other end. It was like the line was tapped. "And what's stopping you? You had your chance."

"It's so easy, anybody could do it. All you do is walk around carrying a bag. Everybody knows how to put one foot in front of the other."

"Then why don't you do it?"

"I would if they let me. Ever hear of Women's Lib? Talk about easy. You just carry around a bag and hold that little flag."

My mom hung up the phone. "You're all set," she said to me. She then leaned into the den and said the same to Matthew.

I turned back to Renee. "Hold on, wait a minute. They did ask you. You said you wanted to be a hostess."

"Yeah, well I didn't realize caddies got paid."

"I'm not doing it for the money."

"Sure you're not. Why else would you?"

"Because they asked me."

"Get real."

Megan was licking one of the beaters as my mom returned to the counter.

"Besides, they said getting paid is no guarantee. If you added up all the hours and the effort, most people would realize the pay wasn't very good. I could make more mowing lawns."

"That's more than a hostess."

"All you have to do is sit around and fetch drinks. They'll even let you sit under an umbrella."

"I'm a volunteer. It's supposed to be easy."

"You had the chance, and you said, no."

"You're just so lucky." She stomped out of the kitchen.

Matthew was still glued to the dazzling screen. He was bobbing and weaving with the game controller. "Nobody better be licking the beaters."

After dinner, I overheard my mother on the telephone. "I have no way to get them there." I pieced together enough of the conversation to realize that she was talking with my uncle. "Megan's ballet rehearsal is the same time. She's been practicing for weeks. I can't miss it."

After a pause I heard her continue. "That would be great," she said. "It's really the only way they'd be able to do it. And I know they want to."

That was two weeks ago. Technically, I guess that's where the story began. The whole thing could've fallen through at that point. First off, the Secret Service could've decided I was a security risk and denied me access from getting anywhere near the President.

But that didn't happen.

Next, I guess I could've turned down the chance to caddy when the idea was first suggested. But what else was I going to do? I couldn't say no to something everyone else seemed to be so eager for me to do. My mom went on and on about how it was an opportunity of a lifetime and that not too many people ever got a chance to caddy for a President. I had caddied before, and felt I could do a good job.

And after hearing the telephone conversation, it appeared that the whole thing hinged on us somehow getting to the golf course. And thanks to Uncle Charlie's offer of a ride, the final obstacle was hurdled. And that's how the whole thing got started.

But since most of the story takes place in one day, the real beginning of this story should probably begin the morning of Sat-On-A-Turd-Day.

Uncle Charlie was at our house early that day.

3

Racing towards the car, Matthew yelled out, "Shotgun." He reached the passenger's side door ahead of us and lifted the handle. When nothing happened, he turned back in our direction. "I called shotgun." He kept his hand on the knob as if it would hold his claim. Like magic, the door locks popped. Matthew tugged the handle once more, and this time it worked. He slid into the leather seat, squirming and spreading out his arms and legs to engulf the luxurious space. By the time we all buckled up and Uncle Charlie eased out of the driveway, Matthew had fiddled with every button and knob within his reach. "What's this one for?"

"That's a seat warmer," Uncle Charlie said.

I pulled down an arm rest in the spacious backseat to separate myself from Renee. A wire ran from the earplug underneath her curls to a transistor radio in her hand. She retreated to a corner and thumbed the toothy dial. I'm sure she wanted to be off the hook from any conversation.

Matthew was raising, lowering, and tilting the front passenger seat in every direction. "What's this one for?" He was taking a shoot first, ask questions later approach.

All the locks snapped down.

I understood Matthew's excitement. Uncle Charlie's car was something different. In the station wagon, we had to crank the windows, fiddle with door handles, and lift knobs to unlock. Some of the knobs were cracked. Screw threads were all that remained on others. It was like Matthew had four arms. His hands touched everything. I felt an impulse to join him. But I controlled the urge. I was hoping to set a better example. I was shooting for a level of maturity.

Mathew's finger went towards the air. "What's this one for?"

"That's the sunroof," Uncle Charlie said.

Matthew reached towards the dash.

Before he could smudge another button with his greasy fingerprint, Uncle Charlie said, "Don't touch that one."

Matthew pulled back. "Why?"

"That's the ejector button."

"Ejector button?"

"Yeah," Uncle Charlie said. "It'll toss you out." I detected a little annoyance in his voice.

"Unhuh."

"Take a chill pill, Matthew," I grabbed his seatbelt and pulled, pinning him back to the seat. "Stop touching stuff."

Matthew glared back at me. After a few seconds, he cocked his head to the side and looked up at Uncle Charlie. "How many horses you got in this baby?"

Uncle Charlie raised an eyebrow. "Horses?" He smiled while keeping focus on the road. "Where'd you come up with that?"

I wondered the same thing. But then I figured Matthew had picked it up from the gear-head clan on the other side of our backyard fence. He had been hanging out there lately. Their potholed driveway was the permanent home of a rusting Chevrolet frame and an assortment of extracted oily parts. The propped-open garage door looked like a cave entrance. Tailpipe rumblings perpetually echoed from the bowels.

"I didn't come up with it." Matthew was confident as a pit crew mechanic. "I know all about cars. What's the horsepower?"

"I'm not exactly sure." Uncle Charlie glanced over at him. "But it's enough."

As we glided down the road, it felt like I was riding in a limo. Of course I had never seen the inside of limo, but I could guess what it would be like. There was enough legroom in the back for a refrigerator and a TV. While you were at it, you could put in a wooden box for cigars and a safe to stash away bags of diamonds and wads of moolah. And the sunroof. That's what I wanted to see opened. I wanted to stick my head out and feel the breeze. I wanted to wave at everyone as we left the neighborhood. I wanted to yell at 'em to get their attention. Then they couldn't miss the fact that it was me riding around in style.

There was one problem with the backseat; it was difficult to be a part of the conversation up front. There was no use talking to Renee. So, I leaned forward and hugged one of the leather headrests. "You know I worked a few days this summer as a caddy?"

"Your mom told me," said Uncle Charlie.

"Well, I've been thinking," I said. "I might try it again next summer. Maybe it'll be a little better if I can move myself up the list."

Uncle Charlie nodded.

"I'm hoping to pick up a few pointers today," I said. "I figured Major could teach me a few things."

Again, Uncle Charlie nodded. "He'd be a good teacher."

I decided to push a little further. Even plant a seed so to speak. "You know," I said, "I've been thinking. When Major decides to retire, maybe I could take over for him."

"There's an idea." Uncle Charlie looked over at me. "I never thought about something like that. That would be nice."

Satisfaction flowed through my veins. My one goal for the day had been achieved. I had tossed around the idea in my brain and fretted over how to bring it up. I wasn't sure how or when I would shed some light on it. And just like that, it was out on the table. Even before we got to the golf course. Better yet, it was met with a positive response. I leaned back feeling confident.

The contentment lasted only a few seconds. Before we even traveled a few hundred feet Uncle Charlie turned the table over. "But you don't want to be a caddy," he said, looking at me through the rearview mirror. "They're basically a bunch of bums."

I was surprised. Caught off-guard.

Renee yanked the wire from her head. "Is Major a bum?" I heard faint music from the earplug.

"No." Uncle Charlie shook his head. "Of course not."

"So, then," Renee said. "Not *all* caddies are bums."

She was giving Uncle Charlie the same business she was always giving me. If I ever was to say, "The sky is blue," Renee would argue. "No it isn't. Not all the time it isn't. When it's cloudy, the sky is white and gray. At dusk and dawn, the sky can be pink and orange. And at night, the sky is black." Usually at this point, I'd give up. I had learned it was much easier to just sit back and let her think she was always right. I knew it was a battle not worth fighting. One I couldn't win.

"Okay," Uncle Charlie said. "I get your point."

At first, I figured Uncle Charlie knew better than to be roped into a debate with Renee. I even wondered if she was actually arguing in my favor.

"When it comes to Sam, it's different," Uncle Charlie continued.

"Oh yeah," Renee smiled. "He's already a bum."

So much for the idea that she was sticking up for me. "Shut up," I said.

"No, no." Uncle Charlie said. "He's family. And when it comes to family, I only give the best advice. And that would be to forget about being a caddy." A few seconds passed. "It's not the kind of life you would want. It's lonely. Most of 'em are drunkards and bums. They get use to the lifestyle, and before you know it they're an old man with no home or any other skills to take their life somewhere else. They're just bums."

At this point, I didn't know what to say. I wasn't going to stir up trouble like Renee. It was no time for a debate. I decided to remain quiet.

Uncle Charlie continued, "Too much time doing nothing. Sharing cheap hotels, eating bad food, staying out half the night. Showing up late with bloodshot eyes. Hung-over. It's not the kind of life you should want. They all think there's some kind of glamour to it, some kind of benefit. They're always gambling on something. A different town each week. Not very disciplined. They earn a big paycheck one week and it's blown by the next month. And if they're not making enough money, they start a downward spiral that's hard to dig out of."

Disappointed and with my hopes dashed, I didn't like what I was hearing. When it came to my future, being a caddy was the only idea I had ever come up with. I tried to stay positive. "But what about today?" I finally regained some composure. "What makes a good caddy?"

Uncle Charlie said. "There's basically two rules."

Here it comes, I thought. I leaned forward hoping to catch a significant tidbit. I wouldn't argue my point. I would simply spend the day showing him that I could do a good job. That would have to go a long way in changing his mind.

"Show up and keep up."

"That's it?"

"Pretty simple." Uncle Charlie nodded. "Show up on time. Make sure you're at the practice range or the first tee when it's time. And keep up. Don't leave your player waiting for his clubs in the middle of the fairway or have him standing around empty-handed on the green. If you have to rake a bunker or fix a divot, do it quickly. Always hustle to keep up. It's that simple. Show up and keep up."

Renee pointed the earplug at me. "I told you being a caddy was easy."

"Go back to your music," I said.

She stuffed the earplug back into her brain. "What ever." She curled her lip as if smelling something rank. She then turned towards the window.

"Some people like to add a third rule," Uncle Charlie said. "And that's to keep your mouth shut. Don't speak until you're spoken to. Keep opinions to yourself. Good shot or bad shot, it's best not to say anything. Stay out of the way, and never argue; even if you think it's the wrong club or bad aim. So, show up, keep up, and keep your mouth shut."

It was enough instruction, both dispensed and absorbed, to keep the ride quiet for some time. After that, Uncle Charlie peppered us with some routine questions about how we were doing in school and if we liked all our teachers. At first I figured he was just trying to pass the time. But then I realized that maybe he was working up to something a little more serious.

"How's your mom doing?"

Matthew was bopping around oblivious.

Uncle Charlie looked in the rearview mirror to me.

I leaned forward near the headrest. "Pretty good," I said. "I guess. We have good days and bad."

Uncle Charlie continued to look at me through the rearview mirror. "Everybody getting along okay?"

"Yessir," I said, nodding. I looked back at Renee and thought about a few melees. I would like to blame the eruptions solely on her. I could have brought up her sass, the screaming threats, the ugly remarks, the tears. Stuff like that. How we were holding on by spider silk.

I looked over to Renee. She pointed at her earplug. "My favorite song," she said in a loud voice, closing her eyes while humming and swaying.

How convenient, I thought. I sneered and turned back towards the driver's seat.

"I've told your mom and now I'm telling you," Uncle Charlie said. "Let me know if you need anything."

I reached over and patted him on the shoulder. "I will." I slumped back into the leather trimmings.

I started thinking. What did he want to know? If Uncle Charlie was in the mood of being a sounding board, I could probably come up with something. There was this dream I kept having. It was probably a worthy topic of discussion. The same thing happened kept happening in every dream. I often wondered about it. Each night, in deep sleep, I lost a tooth. Things felt real enough in the dream to believe it was actually happening. At times it was frightening and caused worry, even panic. It was so real, my heart pumped faster. Sometimes I broke out in a sweat. The dream never had any specific setting. It just had the act of loosing a tooth. Sometimes it was a different tooth. Sometimes it was more than one. I could first feel it getting loose in my jaw. It would begin to wiggle. Soon enough it would work itself out of the gum. I could feel both the wiggling and the gap with my tongue. The dream didn't last long. But again, I was convinced it really happened. I even accepted the fact that I'd have to start chewing my food with one less chopper. And when I smiled, there would be an empty space. Waking up was the best part of the dream. Pure elation was felt when I found everything intact. My tongue probed and found no gaps or wiggling teeth. It was a great relief because I would have sworn and absolutely expected the teeth were lost forever. I chomped the uppers and lowers together. I even tested with my finger. What joy it was to find them all sturdy and in place and in working order. I wondered if Uncle Charlie knew what the dream meant. I leaned forward to ask.

"Check it out," Matthew was pointing toward the windshield. The golf course was in view. "A car! Out in the middle of the lake."

Sure enough, as Uncle Charlie drove up the tree-lined drive, I saw the expansive blue pool of water with windblown waves. Streams from a fountain reached heights of nearly twenty feet. Sun rays lit the spraying mist that cloaked the figure with a rainbow aura. Not far from the dancing vapor, a shiny Cadillac floated on the sparkling surface.

"It's sitting on top of the water," Matthew said. "That is so radical."

And, he was right. All four of the rubber tires touched at the water surface making the car appear as if it was actually driving atop the waves.

"That's one of the tournament sponsors," Uncle Charlie said. "They give away the car if someone makes a hole-in-one."

Matthew continued to point. "How'd they get it to float like that?"

"Underwater platforms."

"But how'd they get the car out there?"

"I'm not sure," said Uncle Charlie.

I said, "I bet they float it out there on a boat. You know, one of them ferry boats."

After of few seconds Matthew said, "But how would they get it off the boat and onto the water?"

"Haven't you ever seen a ferry before?" I said. "They got these gates on the end they drop down. Cars just drive right off. I bet they pulled up a ferry boat next to the platform, dropped the gate, and just drove it right off."

"But wouldn't the boat sink if they dropped the gate. Wouldn't it fill up with water?"

"Nah, that's why it's a ferry boat. They don't sink." I thought about Uncle Charlie's car. "Did you win this car by making a hole-in-one?"

"No," he chuckled. "But let's just say I got a good deal."

There was a reason why I had asked Uncle Charlie if he had ever won a car. There was also an explanation of why he knew all there was about being a caddy. There was a reason why he drove a luxury car. I mentioned earlier that if he hadn't agreed to give us a ride, the whole day would have never happened. But there was more. If it weren't for Uncle Charlie, none of us would've gotten the jobs at the Capital City Pro-Celebrity Golf Tournament in the first place.

4

Chuck Green was the reigning U.S. Open Champion. Before capturing the title, he had won a total of six professional tournaments, made the Ryder Cup team twice, and had twelve top-ten finishes at Majors. Chuck Green, as proclaimed by *GOLF* magazine, possessed the perfect swing. Encouraging all their readers to imitate the ideal motion, the magazine printed as a centerfold, a time-lapsed sixteen panel pictorial analyzing the swing from start to finish. Chuck Green was a favorite son in his hometown and was regularly greeted on the streets by longtime friends and well-wishers. Winning the U.S. Open made him a household name around the world. His image was recognizable and valuable enough for a number of corporations to pay him endorsement fees to pitch their products. He had played golf with Presidents and Prime Ministers, Sultans and Kings, Emirs and Premiers, on the best courses around the globe. But among us, he was simply known as Uncle Charlie.

As we slowed to a gate, the power window next to Uncle Charlie glided down. A security guard stepped out of a kiosk. "Morning Mister Green," the guard said, tipping his cap. He pointed towards a hedgerow near the clubhouse. "Right that way." Through the windshield I spotted another uniformed guard waving toward an empty spot. All day, the same guards would fawn over celebrities with friendly hand signals while shunning the wandering minions with stiff-armed redirections.

At this point it should be easy to figure out how I landed the caddying job for the President. It wasn't because I was a standout junior golfer. Neither was I a promising prospect in a pipeline of young hopefuls in some kind of caddy apprentice program. As far as deserving the job, I was no better a prospect than if someone had pulled my name from a hat. It was my good fortune to have been born a relative of Chuck Green. It was that privilege that gave me the opportunity. I made a promise to myself to work hard and do my best. *And please don't do anything to embarrass the family.*

Once the car came to rest, Uncle Charlie opened the glove box, and said to Matthew, "There's a button you can punch." He pointed at a yellow dot.

Matthew gave it a poke and the trunk latch popped. "Heyyyy," Matthew bobbed his head and raised two thumbs. Matthew Parmarelli—his alter ego inspired by Arthur Fonzarelli. I had seen the act countless times. I would swear that Matthew actually thought he was the 'Fonz.' At times, he even called himself the 'Parm.' I think he was actually convinced that he possessed some kind of magical touch. Every electronic gadget and locked entry in our house had been slapped with an open hand or bumped with a closed fist in hopes that they would magically spring to life or fall open. For Halloween, Matthew dressed in blue jeans and a white T-shirt. He slicked his hair in a ducktail. He would bang on the neighbors' doors and greet them with, "Heeeyyy," and "Whoaaaa." He gave them the thumbs up and they showered him with handfuls of candy. Everybody loved it. That is, everybody but me. I was sick of the 'Parm.'

As we stepped from the car, a couple of teenagers carrying programs approached. "Mister Green," they said. "Can we get an autograph?"

Very casually, as if he had done it a million times, Uncle Charlie smiled and nodded. He took a pen from one of them and signed. "There you go fellas."

When witnessing it from the other side, fame was a funny thing. As the teens thanked Uncle Charlie and started hunting for the next celebrity, I thought that being famous was some kind of reward in itself. Some people even sought the spotlight for what they perceived to be the perks that it brought. No more waiting in lines. Endless offers of free stuff. Recognition. Adoration. That's usually enough for anyone to seek out some level of renown. But, it wasn't that way for Uncle Charlie. His fame was more like a byproduct of his success. He seemed to care so little about notoriety that he often turned down invitations to events that some people spent a lifetime clamoring to attain. I even heard that he once turned down dinner with a Senator because he wanted to stay home and watch a basketball game on TV.

I gave Uncle Charlie a head nod. "Your clubs in the trunk?" I figured I could warm-up being a caddy by offering to carry his bag from the parking lot.

"Come to think of it, that's another important rule," he said. "A good caddy always looks out for the bag. Should never let it out of sight. Always know exactly what's in the bag, especially the number of clubs, and never leave it some place that's not secure."

It seemed the rules of being a caddy were constantly expanding. And the latest rule certainly wouldn't be the last.

I grabbed the handle on the golf bag and lifted. Because it was at an odd angle, I strained some, but got it out to the pavement. I was hoping that when he saw me next to the bag, Uncle Charlie would possibly change his mind about the future. At least, maybe he'd leave the option open.

"Here're your badges," said Uncle Charlie, handing one to each of us. I don't know if I'd actually call them badges. They were pin back buttons. I looked at mine. The tournament information circled the round edge and CADDY was printed in the center. Renee's said VOLUNTEER. Later in the day, I noticed Uncle Charlie's button read, CONTESTANT. He rooted through a box in the trunk and then pulled out three visors. "Here, take one of these," he said, handing one to each of us. The visors sported a corporate logo. "Zach Reyes will get a kick out of you wearing these."

We thanked him. Matthew adjusted the strap and donned the cap. I found a soft spot near the logo and pinned the badge there. It was official. If anyone doubted my status, I would point to the visor and say read this. I am a caddy. Renee looked disinterested. She twirled the hat on a finger. Maybe she didn't want to mess up the hair she had worked on starting at five a.m.

As we paraded from the parking lot, I noticed a line that stretched from a cloth-covered table next to a cart barn. "There's where caddies check-in," Uncle Charlie said. "I'll take the bag from here and see you on the first tee."

As we arrived at the back of the line, Matthew jumped in front of me. I let it slide. I watched as older and taller caddies shuffled toward the table. Those already checked in walked past carrying a two-sided bib. Most of them were in the process of sticking their heads through the trimmed canvas like a football player donning shoulder pads. They were ready for competition. I noticed on front of the bib there was the tournament logo and on the backside was the player's name. I wondered if the nametags were for the benefit of caddies, players, or spectators. A few names were familiar. I wasn't close enough to the table to hear any of the instructions, but I could pretty much guess what was being said. I thought about the past summer and my attempt to be a caddy at a local country club. Although the summer job lasted only three weeks, I remembered the rules and how they were dispensed.

It was a sticky Monday morning when I showed up for the job. I stood outside a shack with a couple of other new hires listening to the caddy master rattle off instructions. Beyond a brief orientation that included the protocol in which bags were to be assigned, he spat out a list of dos and don'ts. The list included: No smoking, No cursing, No gambling, No fighting, No cut-off shorts, and a few others. He made it clear that a single infraction of any of these rules would result in immediate dismissal.

After that, he gave a fine speech.

"All the time, I get calls from parents asking me to give their kid a job." The caddy master bellowed. "Every summer some kid wants to be a caddy. They all have romantic notions. They watch too many golf tournaments and read too many golf magazines. Truth is, the job is far from glamorous." The speech sounded rehearsed. "You'll learn soon enough that being a caddy is hard work. Half the kids won't last more than a few days. If they get a bag, they realize that toting it around in the heat takes a lot of energy. Those that have the strength and energy find out soon enough it takes more than that. It takes some stick-to-it-ness. You can't get discouraged. You have to be dedicated. Good weather or bad weather. Busy or slow. If your player happens to chew you out for stepping in their line or not raking a bunker, or if you keep them waiting for a club, well you have to smile and take it. You'll often be a scapegoat. You'll be a target for blame for things you never did. 'You rattled those clubs in my backswing.' 'I could see your shadow move as I swung.' 'It was your job to keep an eye on my tee shot.' So if you're overly sensitive about what others think or say, you're not gonna make it out here. And as for the pay, if you calculated all the hours, and divide it by the fee you earn for making a loop, you'd probably soon find out you're making less than minimum wage. If you think you're gonna get rich carrying a bag, you might as well give it up now. Go find yourself a job at a fast food joint. Although you'll probably find out soon enough that that's no picnic either. Lifeguard. Now, if I was your age, that's the summer job that I'd be aiming for. Sitting poolside on your duff. Under an umbrella. Twirling a whistle on your finger. Looking at the girls in bathing suits. If any of you had any sense, that's the job you should've signed up for. I imagine those guys never break a sweat and are always happy." At the end of his speech, I wasn't sure if he was trying to encourage us to stick around or to quit before we even started.

As we neared the sign-in table at the Capital City Pro-Celebrity Golf Tournament, I was expecting a similar sermon. Instead, it was just a pair of women checking off names and handing out bibs. As they worked, mature oak trees shaded the area keeping them cool. Behind them, the giant doors of the cart barn were locked shut to both hide and secure golf course maintenance equipment. Near the cart barn, I noticed a scraggly man leaning against the rough bark of a tree.

A lady at the table appeared nervous. Her face was pale. She stood and grimaced. She looked like a teacher about to scold the whole class. She planted both hands on her hips. She shook her head, and then said something to the man leaning against the tree.

I couldn't hear what she said. Next I saw her waving a frantic hand as if she wanted to get the attention of someone toward the back of the line.

I turned to see an apparent staff member rushing toward the table. "I apologize," I heard him say. "I got hung up. What's the problem?"

The lady screwed her face into a bunch as if she had just taken a bite from a lemon. She held one hand over her heart and the other over her mouth. She mumbled something. She then removed the hand from her chest and pointed. "Over there," I heard her say, motioning to the tree trunk.

The staff member eased toward the tree. "Shank," I heard him say as he neared the disheveled man. He said something in a lowered hush. Then I heard him say, "What are we going to do?" He lowered his shaking head.

When Shank smiled, his stubbly cheeks widened exposing a gap in his plaque-coated teeth. "I'm waitin' to get a bag," he said with a resolute tone. "I been waitin' all morning." He held onto the tree trunk with one hand and with the other grabbed his waistband to hold up his stained baggy pants. Sweat soaked through the armpits of his wrinkled silk shirt and his bloodshot eyes swayed as he scanned the ground. His hair was tousled. The pink tip of his tongue worked at the empty space that once housed bicuspids. Spittle flew as he pleaded his case. "This just ain't right."

"You were told on Thursday with the rest of the regulars," the staff member said, calmly. "The club was going to be closed this weekend."

"How come Two Bit got a bag?"

"Someone asked for him."

"When I found out Two Bit got a bag, I decided to show up. Nobody asked for me?"

"Nobody."

"But I needs the work. You dig?"

"I'm sorry Shank, but for the last time, there won't be any bag for you today."

Shank pointed towards the table. "That's not what she said." I got the feeling he had waited through the line only to be rejected.

"There's not going to be a debate," the staff member said. "Understand what I'm saying now and move on. Don't go causing a scene that could get you banned. I'm sure you'll want to carry a bag on regular days."

Shank hung his head. He now used both shaking hands to hold up his drooping pants. He began shuffling away. As he walked past me, I caught a scent of stale wine and dried urine.

Maybe Uncle Charlie was right about caddies.

Maybe they were bums.

"What kind of name is Shank?" The guy in front of us turned and said. "That's got to be the worse name for a caddy. Only thing worse would be, Bogey." The guy in front of us was Chip Swanson. I knew he was and will tell you more about him later. "That guy could change his luck by simply changing his name." Chip Swanson nodded and continued, "He should go by, Ace, or Up and Down."

I nodded as if I understood. "Yeah."

But I was still thinking about something else. *Caddies are bums.*

Even so, at least I had a plump assignment at the Capital City Pro-Celebrity. I was to caddy for the President of the United States. And once I got to meet him, I was sure there had to be some kind of status or benefit of that. Maybe some caddies were bums, but others were not. Maybe it all depended on when and where you caddied and what kind of job was being done. Anybody could be a caddy. Even Renee made that fact clear. But it was up to me to be a good caddy.

But what would that take?

What would that mean?

It was something I would have to figure out.

I did know one thing. I had never met a President and never dreamed that I would. If there ever was a time when someone should be on their best behavior, have a clear head, be eager, be trustworthy, or any of those other things a Boy Scout should be, it's when they're about to meet the President of the United States. I tried to straighten and adjust mentally and physically for what was ahead. Solemn—that's the word I was looking for. When meeting the President for the first time, I figured a person should be solemn, reverent, have some dignity. So that's what I was trying to summon up.

Bums didn't have dignity.

Or did they?

5

Before meeting the President of the United States, I met his golf bag. That alone should be some kind of a privilege. And here I was given the chance to lug the noteworthy bag around for eighteen holes. At the first tee, I was allowed inside the ropes. I edged near the presidential bag in a solemn, reverent manner. The tee was surrounded by a wall of people. I waited. As the seconds ticked away, I slowly gained a level of confidence. I took occasional glances at the golf bag. Although it was like a total stranger, for some reason I didn't want the crowd to think I was on a blind date. At first glance, there was nothing special about the bag. I expected more. I thought that perhaps the President of the United States would have a mammoth-sized, imported, leather job with a hand-stitched Presidential Seal. But, the bag was just ordinary. If not pointed out to me, I would've passed it by.

It had a musty smell, like a damp basement. The partitions that divided the cargo space into thirds had a coating of dust. Wooden clubs were separated from the irons in two of the slots while the putter and wedges occupied the third. Wooden clubs were protected with worn leather head covers. Stitched numbers on the wrinkled skin identified what was hidden under the hood. The set of irons were outdated. Later in the day I overheard the

President explaining, "These clubs were the top of the line when they first came out." Despite some ribbing he was taking for the aging equipment and promises that an upgrade would certainly improve his performance, the President remained firm. "I couldn't get rid of these old sticks. I've gotten so use to them. They're comfortable." To make his final point he added, "Better the devil you know."

Around the tee, the mass of spectators continued to swell. Waiting for the arrival of the President produced raw excitement, stirred with anxiety. I looked around at the crowd. It was made up of all kinds. There were freckled faces, wrinkled faces, pimpled faces, bearded faces, and faces caked with cosmetics. There were interlocked fingers and crossed arms draped over bellies, hands in pockets, hands on hips, and hands shading eyes. There were cardigan sweaters and halter tops. There were ponytails, bouncy curls, crew-cuts, and comb-overs. There were all styles of sunglasses. There were golf hats, bucket hats, straw hats, baseball caps, bonnets, tied scarves, visors, and one red bandana knotted pirate style.

I overheard conversations.

"Who's that?"

"Can we go now?"

"Ever been here?"

"Where's all the movie stars?"

"A buddy of mine works the grounds crew."

There were dimpled smiles and open-mouth gapes, tight-jawed squints, nods and swivels, and a few fingers pressed to pursed lips. There were mumbles, giggles, and a rare yelp from an infant. They were holding cans of beer, cups of soda, hot dogs, programs, and several had binoculars draped like necklaces. One person clutched an umbrella. In the distance they were hooting, hollering, clapping, and waving.

"See that dude over there. He's like a kajillionaire."

"I heard he owns half the shopping malls and movie theaters."

"So he's pretty rich?"

"No, he's not pretty rich. He's stinking rich."

Anticipation hung in the air. It reminded me of a parade. First you could hear sirens, then you could see flashing blue lights, costumed characters carrying a banner, the grand marshal, and you knew that once they got to you, it would be a long time before the entire assemblage of floats and bands made their way past. We were in for a long haul, and everyone was ready for it to get started.

Eyes remained focused on the clubhouse double doors. The President was expected to emerge from there.

A good caddy, I supposed, would perform a quick check of the bag. I wondered if I should take an inventory of clubs, golf balls, tees, etc. As much as I wanted to go rifling through the bag, I restrained the urge. I stood straight and thought about all the things one might come across scouring through a golf bag belonging to President of the United States. There would probably be hidden compartments, possibly booby-trapped. Or maybe something like the red phone, a communication device linking him to the free world should a crisis arise. Should the threat level ever rise to DEFCON THREE, maybe a little light would go on. Better yet, maybe the golf bag hid stashed documents that would shed light on a scandal. Then again, maybe items given to the President as he left office were stored inside. For all I knew, he could be carrying around a putter used by Bobby Jones or a secret book of golf tips written by Sam Snead. I stood straight as a guard at Arlington National. Even if I wanted to peek inside the bag, I'm sure the hulking Secret Service agent next to me would've immediately quashed the idea.

The crowd started to shuffle. Those standing on the path surrounding the first tee slowly parted. At first, I thought it was a Presidential Motorcade. But there was no rumbling of motorcycles or helicopters flying overhead. It was just a golf cart. Then I recognized the driver behind the wheel. I couldn't believe it. It was Matthew. In order to see the road ahead, he was practically standing while steering. He was driving Mister Zach Reyes, the CEO. "Right here Matty," Mister Zach said, as the cart came to a stop. "Let's leave her right here." Mister Zach rose from the seat and slipped through the crowd. He made his way toward the tee markers, pulled a soft leather glove onto his hand, and pointed toward Matthew. "Hey, driver," he said. "Grab my driver."

Matthew gave himself a hug. The crowd broke out in laughter. No doubt they had rehearsed the skit. Matthew followed with an impromptu pair of thumbs up and a, "Heeey," from the 'Parm.'

I had met Mister Zach earlier. He was hard to miss in the red, white, and blue patchwork pants that looked like a leftover remnant from the bicentennial celebration. He was part of the group playing with Uncle Charlie and the President. Matthew was assigned as his caddy.

From the get-go I had my doubts about Matthew being a caddy. When I was asked to caddy, I got the feeling no one wanted to hurt Matthew's feelings or make him feel left out. On several other occasions, he had thrown fits about how it was unfair that I got to do stuff and he didn't. So, he was asked to be a caddy too. That's when my doubts started. Matthew was twelve years old and not exactly big for his age. Carrying around a hulking bag for eighteen holes would certainly present a challenge. Not to mention he wasn't exactly good at calculating yardages or reading greens. Of course when Uncle Charlie suggested he join us, I could hardly express any suspicions or objections. I didn't want to be petty or look like a hog. But I felt a sting when I saw him driving that golf cart. I thought it was unfair.

Matthew grinned from ear-to-ear. He stood on the back cart bumper to withdraw a club from the bag. A towel was draped over his shoulders and he was wearing a brand new golf shirt with a logo of Mister Zach's company on the sleeve. The one-size-fits-all caddy bib was big as a tablecloth on him. Front and back flaps hung on him like a sandwich board. He could go to work parading outside a diner promoting the blue-plate special. The strings sealing the flaps together laced around his waist and the top crease reached beyond his shoulders in sharp points that looked like wings. He cradled the club in his arms and paraded past me never looking in my direction. "Here you are Mister Zach." He dabbed at the face of the club with his towel before handing it over.

Matthew was hamming it up. How lucky could he be? He'd landed the cushiest job at the tournament. Getting to drive around in a golf cart, his biggest strain would be withdrawing clubs from a bag. Didn't anyone know he was too young to drive? Maybe I was a little jealous. At that point I wanted to be able to drive a cart myself. Matthew's day as a caddy was going to be like a day at the amusement park driving around a go-kart track. I wanted the same golden ticket.

I heard a recognizable voice, "Hey there, Rook."

I turned to see Major. He had snuck up next to me. "Hey, Major." I nodded and smiled.

"I can't believe how much you've grown. You're almost as tall as me." He put a hand on my shoulder. "Ready to make a loop?"

"Sure."

Major would be like a mentor. He was Uncle Charlie's regular caddy on tour. He had always been kind to me. I remember first meeting him years before at a similar event. Major took time to talk to us and even gave us a few used golf balls from Uncle Charlie's bag. "You should be all right," he said. "The President's not a bad golfer."

I shrugged. "I hope so."

"Better make sure you have a first-aid kit handy," he said. "You know, maybe a few bandages to stop the bleeding. The President's been known to occasionally pepper the crowd."

I raised both eyebrows.

"Don't worry," Major said. "I'm just yanking your chain. You'll do fine. I'll be around to help. I know CPR."

"Thanks."

"There he is!" A kid in the crowd called out. "There's the President."

A handful of Secret Service agents dressed in grey flannel suits along with a small army of uniformed police officers extended their arms to create a tunnel through the crowd. The President pushed his way down the runway as the onlookers pressed closer. Some of them extended a hand hoping to make physical contact. A few of the hands got shaken. Maybe it was an old campaign habit that kept him cheerful among the constituents. A few other onlookers extended programs and golf hats pleading for an autograph. The requests seemed to be waved off. I heard someone in the crowd mumble, "Says he'll sign at the end of the round." Now out of office and no longer needing the votes, I got the feeling the President could do without the intimacy. I certainly didn't get the feeling he was about to lift a baby from a mother's arms and cover it with kisses.

Once inside the ropes, the President flailed his arms as if he were set free from a cage. He seemed to breathe easier in the open space. I recognized him immediately. I had seen his face plastered all over television and the newspapers. His portrait appeared in history books at school. His image was familiar as the Bumble Bee Baker. But, seeing him in person was different. I expected him to be taller. But, he was ordinary in size and wore a drab green sweater and light brown corduroy pants. He was about as flamboyant as John Boy Walton. He walked directly to Uncle Charlie. "How are you, Chuck?"

Uncle Charlie smiled and stuck out his hand. "Doing fine, Mister President."

I watched as the President shook hands with Mister Zach the CEO and baseball legend Ernie Banks. "Looks like we got a great day for it," I heard the President commenting.

I stood tall, both hands locked to the top of his golf bag. As the President approached, Uncle Charlie said, "This is my nephew, Mister President." Uncle Charlie placed a hand on my shoulder. "Sam Parma."

The President stuck out his hand. "Nice to meet you, son."

I shook his hand. Funny thing, I wasn't too nervous. "Nice to meet you, sir." I got the words out in a fairly calm manner.

The President glanced at his golf bag, slipped the head cover off his driver, lifted it from the bag, and then turned away. I wasn't really paying attention with the hoopla and all, but as he walked away, I realized he had spent only a few seconds near me. He didn't ask for any tees or golf balls or for any advice on where to hit the tee shot. He made the club selection on his own and lifted it from the bag without my assistance. I heard the President say, "We ready?"

I guess it made no difference at that point. I felt pretty good. I had shaken hands with the President of the United States.

Uncle Charlie nodded. "Sure thing, Mister President."

At this point, a man wearing a coat and tie raised a bullhorn and announced the players in our group. He ended with, "Play ahead, gentlemen. You're clear to go."

Tee shots were made and I matched strides with the President down the first fairway. I used the word down as both a description for the direction forward and for the change in elevation. I could have just as well used the word descended because of the sloping terrain. The clubhouse was at the highest point. A climb was required to get home on both the ninth and eighteenth holes. I kept in mind the second rule about keeping up and remained within an arm's length to the President. We made it together to the waiting ball. I stood the bag.

"So, Farmer," the President said, spying the open green ahead of us. "You a good golfer?"

"I'm okay," I said, shrugging my shoulders. "I guess." I was tempted to go into more of an explanation of how little golf I really played. But the rule about keeping my mouth shut popped into my brain so I cut short the response.

The President shook the top of the bag and peered into it. Without asking for advice or even looking in my direction, he pulled an iron and hit a decent approach shot to the first green. As the President continued toward the hole, I scrambled ahead to retrieve the divot and stomp it back into the bare patch. Maybe that's why he called me, Farmer?

Thinking about the rules of being a caddy, I wondered if there were specific rules to follow when caddying for the President. Was there a special towel that I was to use in wiping clods of dirt from the clubface? Was there a special ceremony I was supposed to use in replacing divots torn from the earth? For this wasn't just any regular dirt on the club or sod flying through the air, it was created by the President of the United States. It was Presidential.

The iron club had been propped on the lying bag. The President was well ahead before I was able to grab them both. I had to break into a trot to keep up.

Standing on the collar of the green, the President looked over at Mister Zach and said, "Looks like I got the quiet one."

Mister Zach said, "Probably just a little shy or something."

It was something alright. I was doing my best to follow the rules. I just smiled and shrugged my shoulders.

The President grabbed the rim of his golf bag. "Okay Farmer," he said, "I think I'll use the pitching wedge." He pulled the club from the bag, took a few swipes through the blades of grass, and then chipped the ball onto the green.

So far, it seemed like the President preferred a relaxed, informal affiliation with his caddy. He knew how to foster working relationships so I wouldn't bother trying to correct his misconception of me being shy. But the more I thought about it, the more I wanted to make sure he got my name right. But how could I go about that? Who was I to correct the President of the United States? Since he hailed from a Midwestern state, maybe he liked to call folks working around him, Farmer. Maybe it was like Major calling me Rook. If the President wanted to call me Farmer, maybe I should just live with it. I'd answer to anything. But I figured the time was right to set the record straight. There was no reason to answer to a wrong name for the next four hours. It was a simple misunderstanding. I cleared my voice. "My name is Sam Parma, sir, P-A-R-M-A. Not *Farmer*."

He slid the pitching wedge back into the bag and slapped me on the back. "Sorry son. I meet so many people." He kind of grimaced. "I sometimes lose track."

Maybe he thought I was a smart aleck. I guess that was possible. I just nodded. The rule about keeping my mouth shut wasn't so simple after all. Interpreting the rules of being a good caddy seemed to vary for each person. I guess ultimately it was up to me to decide when I was supposed to follow the rules or when someone else might expect me to bend them a little. It was possible that some people had rules completely different from others.

The President pulled his putter from the bag, turned, and walked away. It was a rough start to a long day. I hoped there would be plenty of chances ahead to smooth it out.

6

It was on the par-3 third hole that I noticed all the cameras. About twenty yards in front, on the right-hand side of the tee, a horde of convex glass lenses stared in my direction. They were like a flock of flamingos lifting their heads from the water. The giant eyes had a smaller black circle in the center just like a pupil. The camera, about the size of an animal cracker box, hung at the end of the cone-shaped telescope. Photographers pressed an eye to the box and readied a finger on top while the other hand twisted the bazooka barrel into focus. Although they were twenty yards away, I imagined they had enough zoom power to count each pimple on my chin.

The cameras were aimed in my direction, but I was not the target. Uncle Charlie and Ernie Banks were worthy of some attention, but the media horde was in place for the President of the United States. They wanted to capture his image. It wasn't everyday that he visited our town. As a matter of fact, it had been two previous administrations when it happened last. Since I stood right next to the President, I couldn't help but be aware of the clicking cameras. It was another reminder of his importance and the opportunity handed to me. With so many snapshots being fired off, there was a high likelihood that some of them would capture my image. I had never thought about the limelight that came with the job. And the more I thought about it, the more I realized that everyone watching your every move may not be such a good thing. There was no place to hide. The thousands of spectator eyes were enough to make me a little nervous. And now I started thinking about commando photographers out to permanently chronicle my slightest misstep. I covertly cruised closer to the dangling rope and propped the golf bag in front of me. I lowered my head so that the visor blocked the sun. With a thumb nail, I dug at a zit on my chin.

I heard a whispered voice. "What do you think here, Sam?"

I looked to my left. The question didn't come from the President.

It was Ernie Banks.

"Well, Mister Banks," I said, hesitating slightly. "I'm not sure." It wasn't a very snappy response.

"Uh huh." Ernie Banks smiled. "So you're keeping all your tips for the President a secret are you?"

"Oh, no sir." I shrugged my shoulders and smiled.

Ernie Banks patted me on the shoulder. "And what did I tell you about calling me Mister Banks?"

"Yessir," I said. "I mean, sure, Ernie." As we were introduced on the first tee I had first called him Mister Banks. He promptly informed me that the only person he knew named Mister Banks was his father and that I should call him Ernie. He was about the nicest famous person I had ever met.

I didn't want to ruin the moment by saying too much. Or maybe it was because I was in awe. Ernie Banks was one of the best shortstops ever to play in the big leagues. He spent his entire career with the Chicago Cubs. He played in the All-Star game fourteen times, racked up 2,583 hits, was named MVP of the league twice, and blasted 512 home runs. Not only was he known for his accomplishments between the lines, but he had the reputation of always being in a cheerful mood on the field, in the locker room, and around everyone he came in contact with. I was learning the reputation held true on the golf course. Ernie Banks was a member of the Baseball Hall of Fame and he knew my name. We shared a conversation on the third hole. And, I wasn't even his caddy.

"I'll be looking for a tip from you before the day is over, Sam." Ernie Banks said as he eased back toward the tee markers.

I hung my head in hangdog fashion. Now there was a kind of guy you'd like to caddy for. I realized that the caddy gig had benefits, that, up to this point, I hadn't realized or counted on. I was rubbing elbows with greatness.

That's when I glanced to my right and saw her for the first time.

Theresa Bellissima was a total fox. Not a fox like Farrah Fawcet, but more of a fox like Rachel Welch. She was the only reason for me to sit up front in Algebra class. I spent lunch period hoping to catch a glimpse of her in the cafeteria. I thought about her in the hallways and knew where her locker was. But the one time I knew I could see her was Algebra class. That's when I made sure to sit up front. And now outdoors, in the sunshine, she was a fox. Theresa Bellissima. Her big brown eyes. My guts were melting. She was smiling. At me.

Do something, stupid.

Say something, stupid.

I flashed a nervous smile. "Hey."

"You're in my Algebra class," she twirled a lock of her hair. "Aren't you?"

She knew me. Since I never really talked to her before, I wasn't sure.

"Um, yeah." I continued nodding like a dope. "Mister Gordon." I just stood there looking dumb as if I were trying to figure out the difference between sine and cosine.

She rolled her eyes and snapped the gum she was chewing. "Goofy Gordon."

"Yeah." I just kept nodding like a dumb bobble-head dog on a dashboard.

"Goofy Gordon is such a goober."

"Yeah."

I glanced back at the tee. Major was counting strides toward the blue tee markers. His lips moved with each step. His last full stride ended up next to Uncle Charlie. Major pulled a small spiral notebook from his back pocket and began flipping through it.

I stole another glance at Theresa Bellissima. Say something, stupid. "Um," I said. "Did we have any homework?" *How brilliant. Couldn't you come up with anything better than that? At least try something funny. Maybe get her to laugh, or smile, or something.*

She looked puzzled and shook her head. "I don't think so."

Maybe I confused her.

What a dope.

I wasn't even paying attention to where Uncle Charlie had hit his shot. But I heard the steel shaft cut through the air and the golf ball go whistling by. The other players, including the President stepped to the white markers. I realized the President was looking for his clubs. I snatched the bag and hurried over. My time chatting up Theresa Bellissima had run out.

The President rifled through the bag, then drew out a club.

Even though our conversation ended, I couldn't help but think about Theresa Bellissima. She was in the crowd. She was watching. How could she miss me? I stood right next to the President of the United States. Things were looking up.

The President turned away. "What do you think, Chuck?"

Uncle Charlie pursed his lips and nodded. "Should play about 156 yards, sir."

"You folks there on the right," the President said, taking a few steps toward the front of the tee. "You may want to move back some." He motioned with an arm. "You may be in more danger than you think." It was the first and only time all day I heard him joke with the crowd. Do I need to remind you about the cameras?

Mister Zach announced, "Get ready to duck or take cover."

As the spectators took a few steps back from the ropes, the President turned to Uncle Charlie, "I wanted to ask you something." He made a few light practice swings and started mentioning pointers he had picked up from other tour players. He said some of the tips worked for him but he had doubts about others.

"Try it this way," I heard Uncle Charlie say to the President. "That's it."

The President made his swing and sent a decent shot toward the green. The crowd was out of danger. I grabbed the strap on the bag and lifted. I glanced over to see if Theresa Bellissima was watching. Okay, I thought, it was time to show your stuff, especially you back muscles, shoulder muscles, and most definitely you biceps. If you muscles happened to have any chance of rippling and swelling to enormous capacity, now is the time to do so. If Theresa Bellissima was watching, she deserved to see my best. I thought about Matthew driving around in the cart. I thought about how lame it would've been if the President's bag was strapped to the back of a golf cart. What if I had been relegated to skipping back and forth to fetch a club? I was no puny kid. Seeing Theresa Bellissima gave me strength. When I realized she was in the crowd, I could've hefted two bags around the golf course. One on each shoulder.

I trailed behind the President as he walked next to Uncle Charlie. I was close enough to hear the conversation. The President said, "What did you think of Palm Desert?"

"It's a great course."

"I played there last month." The President mentioned how he was the guest of the number one ranked golfer in the world. "The place was extraordinary."

Was the President bringing this up to rub it in Uncle Charlie's face? Was he trying to compare his day here, at the Capital City Pro-Celebrity with his experience at Palm Desert? Or was he just making conversation?

"I saw you there," Uncle Charlie said. "You had a pretty good round going didn't you?"

"That's right. I remember seeing your wife. How is she?"

"Fine. Just fine."

"The place was extraordinary."

There was that word again. Extraordinary. The President liked throwing that word around. It's a word that's pretty easy to figure out when you see it written. Extraordinary. Extra-ordinary. Something beyond the ordinary.

The President continued with his story. "The locker room service was extraordinary."

"It's a great venue," said Uncle Charlie.

"All the luxuries you could imagine. All the latest gadgets. Tastiest treats. Anything you could imagine. I like to tell everyone about the locker room. A barber gave me a shave and a hair cut. When we finished the round, not only did they have a table set up with cold drinks and snacks before a shower, but I realized my coat and pants had been pressed, my dress shirt dry cleaned, and my wing tips shined."

"Sounds like they know how to treat their guests," Mister Zach said, walking over after overhearing the discussion.

"Extraordinary," the President said one more time as he pulled the putter from the bag. "I left there looking and feeling better than when I arrived."

And that's when I started thinking about being an extraordinary caddy. Listening to that conversation and taking it to heart was either a tremendous advantage or my downfall. I wasn't sure which. But what I did know was that I wanted to be an extraordinary caddy. Weeks or months from this day, I wanted the President to retell a similar story to a group of dignitaries about his caddy at the Capital City Pro-Celebrity. I only hoped that he would boast about a job performed extraordinarily.

I began to stand taller. If I didn't actually know what I was doing, I'd at least try to make it look like I did. I wondered about that spiral notebook in Major's pocket. I wondered what was on the pages. It obviously made him a better caddy. I wasn't after fame, but I did want to be extraordinary.

7

At six-foot-two, Chip Swanson was an all-city basketball player from Chatsworth Academy. He was also low medalist at the state high school golf tournament as both a sophomore and a junior. Not since Chuck Green, hometown sports reporters declared, was there a better two-sport athlete than Chip Swanson. I knew who he was before we met and could've picked him out in a crowd. But he was even easier to spot today. Chip Swanson was caddying for Ernie Banks.

The President advanced his ball toward the fourth green. I stood nearby in the fairway waiting for others to do the same. Ernie Banks was discussing alternatives with his caddy. Within earshot of their deliberation, I decided to tune in. I figured I could pick up a few pointers.

Ernie Banks rested a hand on top of the bag. "What's it look like, Chip?"

"This is the perfect spot to attack the pin." Chip Swanson reached down and pinched a few blades of grass then tossed them into the air. As the clippings fluttered to the earth, he continued, "The wind shouldn't be a problem either. Maybe even helping a little."

"So, what do you think?"

"I'd try a sawed-down 7-iron. About a three-quarter draw so that it rides the breeze a bit." Chip Swanson held a flat hand to the horizon while visualizing the flight. "You don't want to short side yourself. Land it just past the frog hair and let it track up the hog's back."

These were some fancy words, almost intimidating. Don't ask me to repeat the instructions. Yes, they sounded colorful. And yes, I'm sure they had meaning to someone with a higher level of understanding. But to me, his advice might as well have been, *"You ought to go with a scully nip round the jingle jaw."* I would have understood that just as easily.

My next thought traveled like a boomerang. What kind of colorful caddy lingo did I know? If the President happened to ask, "What do you think, Farmer?" I would be at a loss. My toolbox was empty of flowery terms. The best I could put forward we be something like, "I think you're going to hit it close, sir." Positive reinforcement. That's what I had to offer.

But like I've already hinted, there really wasn't much for me to fret over. The President appeared to expect nothing more from me than to tote the bag.

Ernie Banks hit a nice approach shot and we all moved forward. On the green nothing noteworthy happened. Routine putts were holed in order and we moved toward the next tee.

Major whispered in my ear, "Hand him the driver here." I saw Uncle Charlie already walking away carrying a single club. "After their tee shots," Major said, pointing. "They come right back this way. No sense in carrying the bag all the way down there and then back this way. All they need is the driver."

Before I had the chance to extract the club, the President grabbed the top of the bag and shook it. I stood there looking stupid. He pulled the driver and followed behind Uncle Charlie. I lifted the bag and followed behind Major and Chip Swanson.

"I guess I should've mentioned one more thing," Major said in a louder voice now that we had some distance between ourselves and the crowd.

"What's that?"

"I should've told you before we got this far. Do you know if the President has an extra ball in his pocket? And tees? In case he hits one out-of-bounds."

I assumed a shortcut would make things easier. Again, I was wrong. Not knowing the rules for the shortcut added a layer of difficulty. "I'm not sure," I said, shaking my head. I had no idea if the President had an extra golf ball or tee. I failed to take notice. And it was too late. I missed the opportunity to ask.

Major moved out ahead into the fairway. "You guys can wait here."

I stood next to Chip Swanson in the shade. "Did I hear right," Chip Swanson said. "You related to Chuck Green?"

"Yeah," I said, growing nervous over the fact that I didn't know if the President was stranded on the tee without extra golf balls or tees. "He's my uncle."

"That's cool."

All I could think of at the time was what would happen if by chance the President needed a tee. If he didn't have one in his pocket, he would surely ask to borrow one from someone else. Maybe one of the Secret Service agents carried around a few spares. "Yeah," I said to Chip Swanson. "It's pretty cool."

"You caddy much?"

"I worked last summer at a country club," I said. "And a tournament like this." I started thinking about the possibility of the President hitting his tee shot out-of-bounds. If he didn't have an extra golf ball, I envisioned him and all ten thousand people on the tee flagging me down. They'd all wave and yell for me to run back to the tee with the golf bag. I would certainly look like a fool. It would be proof that I didn't know what I was doing. I tried not to worry about it. "How 'bout you?"

"I don't caddy much," he said. "I'd rather be playing."

That's when it hit me. I was carrying on a conversation with Chip Swanson. He was a couple of years older, taller, and practically a sports celebrity. At school, someone on his level would never bother talking to me. He would pass me in the halls without a glance. But here we were, at the Cap City Pro-Celebrity swapping stories like old friends. "Yeah," I said, "I think I've seen your name in the paper." Truth was, hanging around and being seen with Chip Swanson was almost as good as being associated with Ernie Banks and Uncle Charlie. I looked up at him. "Why aren't you playing today?"

Out in the sunny fairway, Major raised an arm motioning for the players on the tee to proceed. The coast was clear.

"I tried," Chip Swanson continued. "We're members here. My dad talked to a committee. They agree I was a good enough. Maybe a few of them were worried I was too good. Maybe even wind up winning."

A ball bounced by Major and rolled down the middle of the fairway.

I took a few steps up the cart path to get a view of the tee. I could see the President standing and waiting his turn. Chip Swanson continued, but I wasn't completely tuned in.

"But they decided not to invite me. Maybe in a few years they said. But I think they didn't want any chance of a high school guy winning their tournament."

I was able to make out the image of Ernie Banks through the branches. He was addressing a ball on the tee in front of him. He made a swing and his ball soared in our direction. It bounced twice then came to rest in the middle of the fairway. Next up was the President. It appeared to me that he propped his golf ball on a tee. Whether he had to borrow one in advance, I wasn't sure. A silent chant ran through my brain. *Please don't hit it out-of-bounds.* I never rooted so hard for the President all day. *Please hit it in the fairway. Please hit it in the fairway.* I thought about crossing my fingers.

"To show there were no hard feelings, they invited me to be a caddy," Chip Swanson was saying. "I guess I understand. To show I had no hard feelings either, I took 'em up on it. In a few years, when I make the tour, I imagine there'll be committees lining up and begging me to play in all kinds of events like this."

Please hit it in the fairway. The President made his swing. The ball took off from the tee on a low line drive. It wasn't actually well-hit, and I lost it in the air. *Please land in the fairway.* I turned to see Major take a few steps as a ball came to rest a few feet in front of him. The President's ball had stayed in play. I took a deep breath. All the worry for nothing.

Getting out ahead of the tee was supposed to make the job easier. But that wasn't necessarily the case for me. The shortcut created some second-guessing. A bit of confidence drained from my reserves. It did remind me of something. "Major keeps pulling out some kind of notepad," I said to Chip Swanson. "I've been trying to get a look at it. You got a notepad?"

"Nah," Chip Swanson shook his head. "I know this course like the back of my hand."

"I've been wondering what's in it."

"I'm sure just notes on the course. You know, yardages, trouble zones, what club to hit from certain spots. How the wind blows and which way the greens tilt. Stuff like that."

"Sounds pretty useful."

"It probably would be," Chip Swanson said. "But I don't need a notepad for all that stuff. I got it all up here." He tapped at his temple. "I know this place better than anyone."

If you're wondering where Matthew was all this time, you have to remember he drove a golf cart. There was no need for him to conserve time or energy worrying about covering the ground twice. He could do it easily behind a wheel.

Chip Swanson continued, "I've been playing this course my whole life. No one knows it better than me. If you can play this course well, you can play well anywhere. I've won the state a couple of times." I wasn't sure if he was being humble or bragging. "The Cap City is about the biggest event around here. Especially with the President being here. I think those folks on the committee knew I would be a good caddy. They knew I could give some pretty good advice on how to putt the greens, where the out-bounds-markers are, targets to aim for, stuff like that. Not a bad way to earn a few bucks either. And since the club would be closed, I couldn't hustle my normal few bucks from the old men." He paused, probably hoping to see my reaction. When I just nodded, he continued. "I'm not bragging, but I know I've got talent for the game. And it can take me places."

I knew I wasn't as good of a caddy as Chip Swanson. For that matter, I was nowhere near the same league as Major. But I didn't care. Maybe on some level, someone would at least see that I was trying. Just by caddying next to Major and Chip Swanson, doing the same work so to speak, gave me some legitimacy. And once I realized that I wasn't going to have to go running back to the tee looking like a fool, I breathed a little easier.

As for Matthew, it seemed the day would be a breeze for him. I knew I couldn't get by with just being cute. For starters, I was too big and too old. But I didn't mind. I was willing to carry the load like an adult. If anyone asked, I had no problem admitting that I was still learning. And because the job didn't come so naturally, I would even argue that I had to work even harder than someone with tons of experience or God-given talent. To do a good job, I knew I would have to pay attention and learn all I could. Whether that meant coming up with some fancy language that made it sound like I knew what I was talking about, or keeping on eye on the flight path of every shot. While I was thinking about it, keeping an eye on the flight path of every shot was not restricted to just those players within my own group. I was about to learn that golf balls could come flying at you from all directions.

8

Three white orbs dotted the mowed crisscross pattern of the fairway. On the opposite side, Major entered the shadowy forest to search for the wayward fourth. I looked back toward the tee. A sign-bearer was just departing ahead of the group. I could continue to stand there and wait, or I could assist Major with the hunt. I laid the President's bag flat in the first cut of rough and jogged across the fairway. "One go in the woods?"

"Zach Reyes," Major said, kicking at the ground.

"Sorry," I said. "Didn't see it. Should've been watching."

"Don't worry Rook. You're learning."

I had been too busy listening to Chip Swanson and fretting over the President to concern myself with other things. Latest lesson learned: keep an eye on all the players' shots. There was more to be taught.

Major knew that. That's why he was calling me Rook. At first I thought it was because he thought of me as a chess piece. If that was the case, he'd be better off calling me Pawn. Then I thought Rook might be some type of card game, something I would have to play after the round as some sort of caddy initiation. But after a while, I figured out that Rook was short for rookie. I didn't mind the nickname. At least it held out promise that I could get better. A caddy named Rook was better than one called Hapless, or Cranky, or Gloomy. I wouldn't want to be called any of those. Or worse, a name like Bum or Shank.

"By the way," Major said. "The President's tee shot landed on the edge of the fairway, near the cart path."

"Got it," I said. "I left the bag there. Guess I shoulda kept an eye out for everyone."

"You're learning."

Major found the wayward shot and signaled for a marshal to come over and mark the spot. I hustled back across the fairway. The President had arrived and was grasping the rim of the bag he had raised from the ground. He was shaking it to get a glimpse of its contents. I grabbed the strap to let him know that I was there and was keeping up. We both watched and waited. Matthew was nearby sitting behind the wheel in the cart as Mister Zach hacked his ball from the woods. I couldn't tell if it took him more than one stroke to escape. The President drew a club and began taking practice swings. The pot marked fairway was littered with drying divot fragments.

After a second practice swing the President said, "Sure is a beautiful day."

It took me a few seconds to realize he was talking to me. I spat out, "Yessir." I started to say that it was an extraordinary day, but decided to keep my mouth shut.

The President took another practice swing as we waited. Ernie Banks was next to play.

I watched Chip Swanson. He was ahead in the middle of the fairway. He was taking long strides while silently counting them off. He stopped at the waiting golf ball and said to Ernie Banks, "We got 163."

When it came to yardages, I knew the basics. The small shrubs planted on both sides of the fairway measured 150 yards to the middle of the green. I had learned from Major and Chip Swanson how to measure the precise yardage depending on the pin placement. The key was dependent on the color of the flag on the green. They were red, white, or blue, and went in that order. Red being a front placement, white middle, and blue on the back. So, the 150 yard shrub markers from the fairway were only accurate if the flag waving on the green happened to be white. A caddy would have to add or subtract from that yardage depending on whether a red or blue flag fluttered ahead. Once you got that much figured out, you would have to add or subtract the strides, assuming you had good judgment on the length of a single yard, to the 150 already figured for you at the pair of shrubs. I won't even go into how to add or subtract yards depending on uphill or downhill or wind direction and strength. I have included this explanation as a reminder that being a caddy was not so easy.

"With the wind and since it's a little uphill," I heard Chip Swanson saying, "It'll play a buck seventy one."

All the calculations swimming in my head left me dizzy. Chip Swanson made it look easy. He had it down to the exact yard. Before watching him, I was confident. But now, if the President was to ask me for advice on distance, I had doubts about what I could deliver. I hoped he wouldn't ask. Anything I could calculate certainly wouldn't be reported with the same confidence of Chip Swanson. And I knew to forget about trying to fool anybody. A caddy that just threw out rough estimates or took a stab in the dark would certainly be doomed to a short career.

A gaggle of spectators behind us began to squawk. I heard a woman's voice, "Oh my!" A loud man's voice, "What's the big rush?" I looked over and spotted a marshal wearing Bermuda shorts. He lifted the rope, bent under it, and started jogging toward us. He reached the middle of the fairway and then turned back toward the tee. He started waving his arms over his head. He then turned to us and warned, "One coming this way, sir."

A golf ball was bounding in our direction. Someone back on the tee had hit too early. They had either gotten impatient or assumed we were out of range. Hitting into the group ahead was about the rudest thing a person could do on a golf course. I saw the approaching ball as it rolled in our direction. It came to a halt about ten feet from us.

The President kept cool. He smiled and waved to the crowd. "That was a close call," he said. "Thanks for the warning."

The marshal in Bermuda shorts puffed up his chest. He must have felt patriotic. He would probably tell his grandchildren how he had warned the President of danger.

A random unidentifiable voice from the crowd said, "I bet it was a *Republican*." The gathered crowd laughed.

Or did he say *Democrat*? I didn't really know the difference. They both pretty much seemed the same to me.

The President smiled and waved again. He then turned back to golf. The same thing would probably stir up the average guy on the links leading to fist waving curses. Someone hitting into you was an unsettling, rude, and possibly even dangerous situation. But it didn't seem to bother the President. He was a master at maintaining composure.

It was enough to stir the crowd though. A spectator said, "You think that was deliberate?"

Another said, "Where's the Secret Service when you need 'em?"

Pretty soon, different voices flung different opinions.

"Aren't they supposed to step in front of something like that and block it with their body?"

"Maybe that's the caddy's job. He's the one that's supposed to protect the President from golf balls."

"Who's that playing behind them?"

"Such a big-time blowhard."

"I know who you're talking about. Ain't he one of them lobbyists?"

"Wouldn't surprise me if it was done on purpose."

"I thought he was in jail?"

After seeing what had happened, Ernie Banks pulled a handkerchief from his back pocket and waved it in mock surrender.

It took several minutes for the crowd to settle. The wind whipped through the trees. A cloud of dust spiraled from a patch of bare ground. The President finally made a swing and sent his ball towards the green.

Those watching outside the ropes applauded politely, but I could tell the President wasn't exactly happy with the results. First, it was easy to realize he hadn't hit it very well. As the iron face of the club contacted the ball, it sounded mushy. A large divot was cut from the earth. Also, the flight path of the ball was weak and it landed short of where he was aiming. And if those clues weren't good enough, there was more. I could see what the crowd couldn't. The President had a stranglehold grip on the club. I got the feeling he was trying to squeeze the life out of it. I believe it was something apparent only to me. I realized, up close, things were different.

I lifted the bag. The strap weighed heavy on my shoulder as I trudged toward the green. Throughout the day, I would shift the harness from one side to the other. It was one of those commonsense caddy tips that I learned on my own. If one shoulder started to ache, I would shift to the other.

As we approached the green, I watched Matthew slide out of his seat in the golf cart. Chocolate stained the corner of his mouth. He was busy chewing and didn't say anything. Instead, he briefly halted the chomping, closed his eyes, and shot me a spiteful smile. His gestures were louder than words. They said, "While you're sweating it out with the heavy load strapped across your shoulders I'm enjoying a life in luxury and the tasty treats are delicious."

"Look at that little guy go," I heard a lady's voice. "He looks so cute. That uniform swallows him. I'll bet he's going to run five miles today going back and forth." She was falling for the act. "His little legs are just pumping away."

I was close enough to see inside the cart. Blanketed inside a napkin was a hot dog loaded with relish and mustard. A can of soda sweated inside a cup holder. I then spotted an empty candy bar wrapper, a stack of cellophane-wrapped peanut butter crackers, and a box of unopened moon pies. Matthew was working his way through the spoils.

As we stood on the next tee, the group behind us approached. The political bigwig hopped from his golf cart and said, "Sorry 'bout that last one." His voice was as loud as his clothes. White shoes, white belt, white brim hat big as a sombrero. Lime green shirt and tropical colored patchwork pants that could've been a Caribbean quilt. He also wore a phony smile and waved in our direction. "Didn't think I could hit it that far."

The President just nodded with the rest of the players in our group, but the grumbles from the crowd continued. Outside the ropes there was on ongoing debate on whether the long drive that neared the President was launched deliberately. It seemed the spectators weren't going to forget so easily.

"I wouldn't doubt if that blowhard started bragging about hitting into the President—No way that was an accident."

"He apologized. Give him credit for that."

"I don't trust any of 'em."

I wasn't so sure what or who to believe. Politics, it seemed to me, were always like that. You never got the full story behind any politician's true motivation. To what level they would stoop. What promises would be kept or broken. If there was anything genuine about them at all.

The controversy continued to ripple through the crowd. It was a reminder of how closely they were paying attention. No matter where he went, I imagined the President of the United States always had a crowd around him scrutinizing every move. The security, the cameras, the crowds; I felt all the eyes and ears. I certainly didn't think the caddy job would come with such a bright spotlight. But when it started shining, I didn't necessarily dislike it. And when it came to the Big Goof, I would've given anything in the world for no one to notice. But I'll get to that soon enough.

9

I've been a little emphatic about using fancy words here and there. Words like *emphatic*. You can blame my Language Arts teacher for that. She had encouraged me to include such words in this story. She said I needed to add a little color and learn how to say the same thing in different ways. She's gotten me in a habit of consulting both a dictionary and a thesaurus. As you have already encountered a few of them, I'm sure you'll recognize that maybe sometimes I overdo it. And if you're wondering how come most of the sentences make sense with the spelling and punctuation and such, it's because my Language Arts teacher has been helpful enough to mark up different portions. Every now and then between classes and during lunch I've shown her bits and pieces. I kept asking about extra credit and she kept bugging me about writing a story. "Whenever you get the notion," she said to me. "Write down things you think make a good story." It sounded simple enough. "Put your ideas into words," she said. "Just as if you were telling someone about it."

So I started.

Once she looked over a few pages, she told me to keep going. She said she would like to see a little more conflict between the characters, like between Sam and Matthew. I thought there was already plenty of conflict. I also thought there was plenty of conflict going on in my head. She also said there should be more drama built in. She suggested that Sam should seek something from the President like a recommendation letter for college. That didn't sound right to me. So I left that out. I think she doesn't like golf. She also said I should spend a little more time describing what I look like so the reader can have an idea of the person they're rooting for. But I figured what I looked like wasn't all that important. Why spend all that time mentioning that I looked exactly like Arnold Schwarzenegger?

I'm hoping that the story is good enough for some people to even like it. For the most part, I've gone back to make sure her corrections were included. The help may be obvious in some of the fancier writing parts.

And as for anyone wondering why I haven't included any curse words, there's a reason for that too. I don't think it has anything to do with the story. I've noticed that some books, even the ones we're supposed to read in school, included a sprinkling of obscenities. Teachers always told students that it was okay because it added a realistic flavor. But I thought it was just an easy way to get attention. Most kids would read anything if you told them it had curse words in it.

Maybe I'll go back and slip a few in. But then again, like I said, I don't think it has anything to do with the story. I certainly wouldn't use words like that around my mom, my uncle, or for that matter, the President of the United States. But I couldn't exactly rule out using curse words when it came to what I was thinking.

As we walked down the next fairway, I was close enough to Chip Swanson to overhear him mixing with a few guys in the crowd. There were three of them. They were well-dressed and could've either been friends from school or the country club. "Hey Chipper," one of them shouted through cupped hands. "You'd be three under by now." Chip just waved. "Hey Swanson," another one of them called out. "Did you tell Ernie Banks you were a White Sox fan?"

As our pace slowed, Chip Swanson made his way over to his pals. One of them mumbled something I couldn't hear. Chip Swanson turned in my direction and pointed with his thumb.

"That's Sam Green," he said. "Chuck Green's nephew." The guy mumbled something else and the others laughed.

"Hey Chipper," another one said loud enough for me to hear. "I think you could take Chuck Green."

Now that one really got me. I didn't care that older guys, probably seniors, looked down on me. I was familiar with how seniors treated sophomores. I didn't even care that Chip Swanson got my name wrong. But when it came to Uncle Charlie, I couldn't let them get away with such a ridiculous claim. I curled my lip and made a noise. "Hrrmph."

Chip Swanson just smiled. He played along with his pals. It was like he knew he was getting ribbed. "Who let you guys in here?" He said. "Did you ride in the bread truck with the Bumble Bee? Hey Finny, save up enough wrappers?"

It took me a few seconds to realize what he was talking about.

The Bumble Bee Baker was known by everyone in town. The cartoon logo, complete with a bulging yellow and black striped midsection, transparent humming wings, smiling face, and antennae protruding from a chef's hat, appeared everywhere. The Bumble Bee promoted baked goods in the grocery aisle and could be spotted resting on the seatbacks of bus stop benches, on sheet metal signs attached to outfield fences on baseball diamonds, under concession stand counters at public swimming pools, and wrapped around their delivery trucks.

As a sponsor of the tournament, the Bumble Bee Bakery offered anyone willing to save five bread wrappers a free general admission ticket good for one day at the Capital City Pro-Celebrity. All you had to do was bring the proofs of purchase to the tournament and wait patiently in line to redeem a free ticket. It was a win-win situation for everyone. Tournament organizers longed for a large crowd and the promotion brought out folks that otherwise may have been unable to attend. And to make it a win-win-win, the prominent rectangular cardboard ticket was one more outlet to display the Bumble Bee logo. The catchy jingle, broadcast on radio and TV, targeted consumers of all ages. The words and music lingered in your brain. A little banjo twang accompanied a folksy blending of mellow voices. "Wholesome nutrition for a teaspoon of money," the singers harmonized. "Baked locally each day with a touch of honey."

The guys ribbing Chip Swanson responded with an off-key rendition. "With a touch of honey." On their waists they wore shiny plastic badges with the word, MEMBER. It allowed access to the clubhouse during the tournament. They were kind of funny singing the jingle.

I took a few quick strides to catch up to the President. We crossed a bridge to a remote putting green. The smooth surface of the water was like a mirror reflecting two worlds. The upside down world had the same footbridge, greenside bunker, tall pines, and sloping sod to its border.

Around the green there wasn't enough room for the crowd. They were not allowed across the bridge. The separation occurred several times during the day, whenever there were tight borders of water, woods, or fences. All the action could be viewed by the spectators, but it was from a distance. It was during these times, out of earshot of the populace, that casual conversation between players was easy to pick up. I wasn't exactly a fly on the wall, but more like the idiot hanging on to a golf bag.

"I read your book the other day," Ernie Banks said to Mister Zach. "I was on the redeye from the west coast and couldn't sleep."

"I hope it didn't put you to sleep," Mister Zach said, smiling.

Zachary P. Reyes was President and CEO of a large electronics conglomerate. Among friends and fellow business tycoons he liked to be called a folksy Zach (rhymed with Jack). On talk shows and when pitching his products, he liked to be known as Mister Zee. But employees in worldwide manufacturing plants and distribution channels as well as those wearing coats and ties in the corporate tower and around the boardroom addressed him as Mister Reyes. A survivor of quadruple bypass surgery, some of his detractors referred to him as Zach, Zach the Heart Attack. His business book, *Ex-Zach-ting Excellence,* spent twenty weeks on *The New York Times* bestseller list. Mister Zach Reyes was an avid golfer and carried a fifteen handicap. Realizing a large portion of his customer base shared an interest in golf, he promoted the company through numerous tournament sponsorships. He also maintained a stable of tour players to endorse his products. Uncle Charlie was one of the horses in that barn.

"No. No," Ernie Banks said, shaking his head and smiling. "I enjoyed the baseball analogies. Lots of folks in business like to use baseball analogies."

Putts were holed and our group strolled to the next tee. The water hazard continued to separate us from the crowd. Uncle Charlie prepared for his drive from a back tee. The three other players chatted while waiting their turn at the forward tees.

"Always be a home run hitter," Mister Zach said, rambling off what sounded like a catchphrase. "I'm always on the lookout for the home run hitter. The guy with the big idea that's going to drive in all the runs. Make the big profit. I don't need any single hitters in my company."

The President chimed in, "How 'bout that Mr. October?"

"Three home runs in one game."

"Better yet, a World Series game. Extraordinary."

"Exactly the kind of man I'm looking for," Mister Zach continued. "Like I said, I don't need any of those guys that occasionally slap a weak dribbler through a gap in the infield. They're okay for some companies. They get on base, and yes, if they do it often enough, they're of some use. But in my organization, nothing's proven more successful than good old power. The guy that can change the game with one mighty swing."

"Some of those guys strike out a lot too," Ernie Banks said.

"I allow for a little risk taking if the reward has some value, but if my home run hitter starts striking out, it's time for me to change batters."

The President jumped back in. "My experience leads me to see it a little differently," he said. "I don't mind the single hitters. They're usually the ones that think first about the success of the team. My favorite guy in the organization is the one that comes up with the bases loaded, and instead of swinging for the fence, he's thinking about doing whatever it takes to get the runner home. Especially if there're two outs and it's late in the game. My guy's the one that'll do anything not to kill the rally. Not make the last out. My guy has one thing in mind. Success of the team. A single with two outs and the bases loaded is a glorious thing. If not a single, work the pitcher. Earn a walk. If not a walk, then think about that fastball zooming in high and tight. If it were important enough, the right guy wouldn't duck out of the batter's box. He would stand his ground. He would get the job done by taking that flaming fastball in the ribs. You can keep your home run hitters. I want the guy willing to take one for the team."

I thought about what he was saying. Maybe I should've stepped in front of that wayward shot barreling down on us back in the fairway. Okay, maybe I'm exaggerating a bit by saying it was barreling down on us. But if I had shown I was willing to protect him at any cost, it certainly would've shown the President that I was the kind of guy capable of being his caddy. It would be the kind of story that he would tell others in the future. I could hear it now, "I once had an extraordinary caddy," he would say, lolling away time on a golf course. "He stepped out and took a golf ball in the coconut for me." He would rub his chin, fondly recalling my service. "That caddy was extraordinary."

We crossed the bridge and rejoined the crowd now lining the fairway. I had baseball on my mind. Approach shots were made to an elevated green. When we got to the putting green, spectators were five deep up a hillside. They remained quiet enough for me to hear Chip Swanson standing behind the putter blade of Ernie Banks.

"This one's a real slider," he said. "Play it about three balls to the high side. It falls off past the hole, so careful with the pace. Let it die over the lip. You may want to leave the head cover on the putter."

I tried to make sense of the elaborate instructions. I wasn't sure if all the fancy caddy advice had anything to do with the outcome. It sounded great but I hardly understood it. Good thing the President hadn't asked me for putting advice.

Ernie Banks made his stroke and the putt ran out of steam just short of the hole.

Mister Zach was next. He faced a ten foot putt for birdie. Even better news for the team was the fact that it was on a hole in which his handicap afforded him an extra stroke. The team score was in great need. Mister Zach seemed to thrive on the importance. He paced back and forth several times trying to uncover the likely path for success. It looked like he was *Ex-Zachting Excellence.*

Since the President had already finished with a bogey, he was regulated to cheerleading. "We need this one," he urged, standing next to me on the fringe.

Assuming my duties were no longer needed on this hole, I figured it was a good time to relax. I decided to give my mind a rest and started thinking about baseball. All the talk about home run hitters and singles hitters placed me back on the diamond. But instead of the dusty Rotary Park field of the past summer, I found myself dressed in pinstripes in front of a stadium crowd.

Mister Zach got Matthew involved. "What do you think here, caddy?"

Matthew handed over the golf ball he had wiped clean. He squinted and motioned with his hand. "I think it goes a little this way." The moist end of the towel draped over his shoulder reached the ground.

"That's my boy."

I needed to escape. Back in the stadium on the diamond, I could hear the urging crowd. I had just lined a shot to the corner in right field. I gasped for air as I rounded second base. I looked for the third base coach. I spotted him with both arms raised. "Hold up," he was instructing. But by the time I was within fifteen feet of the bag, he dropped his arms and yelled, "Get down." A throw was on the way.

Mister Zach addressed his putt. Matthew stood to his side with both fingers crossed.

Back on the base path, I started falling forward. My helmeted head stretched beyond my feet. Once I reached the point of no-return, I went ahead and took the dive towards the now-blocked base. My chest bounced off the hard dirt. I looked for a spot, reached around a pair of stirrup socks, and tagged safely.

Mister Zach stroked his ball and it rolled toward the hole.

The pair of cleats blocking the base leaped. The throw was high. The third base coach was yelling, "Go. Go." I looked up to see him below the plastic bill of my helmet. He was now waving one arm in windmill fashion urging me to continue. I could taste the dust as I sprang to my feet. With a fresh stain on the front of my uniform, I started digging for home.

Mister Zach's birdie putt fell into the hole and the crowd let out a cheer.

I crossed the plate and heard the same noise. Applause. Whoops and whistles. Clapping hands. Recognition for my hustle around the base paths. A job well done.

Matthew, with the oversized bib, swiveled his hips hula-style. "Mister Zach," he said, smiling and shimmying. "Look at this. It's my birdie dance."

"That's my boy," Mister Zach said, slapping him on the back as they left the green. "I want to see that dance again."

I lifted the bag to my shoulder. The heavy load brought me back to reality. At least I made good with the time. A little daydream was better than watching Matthew doing the birdie dance. And before you go and think that there's no way I've ever displayed that kind of speed around the base paths, let me remind you, it was a fantasy. Better yet, it was my fantasy. And why would I picture myself slow as a snail in my own daydream? And although the vision was somewhat like a home run, maybe it should've been more to the President's liking. Maybe I should've envisioned myself taking a fastball in the cranium. But that wouldn't be much of a fantasy either. And as for daydreaming while caddying, if only I could've told myself at that point to be careful not to do it again. It probably would've kept me from committing the Big Goof.

10

I had lugged the President's golf bag for nine holes. The deadweight draped over my shoulders felt like a barely-breathing body pulled from a burning building. I swiped the sweat from my forehead with a finger. I can't say that I was anywhere near exhausted, but the thought of working for that icy glass of lemonade and the five dollar bill signifying the end of a lawn job entered my mind. Not quite delusional, I had a thirst quenching thought. Maybe the Kool-Aid man would come busting through the woods tearing bark from trees, overturning mounds of shrubbery, and kicking through flower beds. He'd be so full of cherry-flavored Kool-Aid that it would be splashing over the brim. Ice cubes jostling behind his big smiling face. Glass sweating. Red liquid relief. If that had happened next, it would make for a story categorized in the realm of fantasy. But this was not a mythological, mystical, supernatural story. No werewolves. No vampires. No wizards casting spells. So that of course meant that the Kool-Aid man didn't materialized anywhere beyond my brain.

It wasn't exactly the Kool-Aid man, but relief was in sight. I spotted Renee on the tenth tee. She had on a flowery green apron with pockets in front. She stood clutching two dripping bottles of water behind an open cooler lid. It was one of the rare times I saw her smiling. As our group funneled through the ropes, I heard her saying, "Would anyone like something to drink?"

Uncle Charlie stopped. He placed a hand on Renee's shoulder and said something I couldn't hear. Renee nodded, smiled, and then handed out a few cold drinks.

The tenth hole was a par 3. A parking lot left of the tee was giving off a wavy mirage from the heat. On the right was a lake. Along the shore, in the windblown wake, a pair of mallards chattered and splashed with their wings. A clump of cattails provided cover for freshly-hatched minnows. Insects spiraled above. The pumping fountain offshore spewed white droplets high into the air. The manmade shower sang like a perpetual torrential chorus. On the surface next to the fountain, in a rainbow halo of mist, the Cadillac floated.

I slid the bag from my shoulder and sidled up to the cooler. Without Renee's assistance, I plunged an arm deep in the icy water. My hand went numb as I dug and pulled out a can. I retreated to a shady spot with the bag and popped the can top. I gulped half the can's contents without stopping. The icy grape soda burned my throat as it went down. I glanced over to the crowd and saw Theresa Bellissima. The dangling yellow rope quivered between the silver rings on her tan fingers. Her nails were painted a bright red. She nodded and smiled in my direction.

Even the dumbest of fools knew this was an opportunity. I tried to think of something to say. "What do you think?" I said, leaning in her direction. It was the best I could come up with.

"You won't believe who I just saw," she said, gushing the name of some Hollywood movie star. "I couldn't believe how short he was."

"Really?" I said. "I didn't know he was out here."

"Yeah," she said, reeling off a few other names. "I hope I get to see them too."

"Cool," I said, nodding.

A marshal raised his arms to quiet the crowd as Uncle Charlie took aim from the back tee. He made a swing and the ball sliced through the air.

I said, "Gotta go."

Theresa Bellissima smiled and whispered. "See you later."

I could only hope that that was true. I lifted the bag and edged closer to the President. He was standing between the white tee markers. Uncle Charlie joined us. The President tapped him for another quick swing tip.

Away from the crowd I saw Major standing next to the golf cart parked near the lake. He was drinking from a bottle of water and talking to Matthew. He had the notebook out and was flipping through the pages. Matthew, still sitting behind the wheel, was looking up at him and talking. I couldn't believe what I was seeing. All day I had waited for the perfect opportunity to ask Major about the notepad. And there was Matthew having all the helpful contents showered on him. I wasn't close enough to hear what was being said. As the President conversed with Uncle Charlie, I drew closer to the cart.

"They use a helicopter," I heard Major saying. "See, they wrap this big nylon strap around each of the four tires and tighten it to a point. They gather it with a hook, you know, kind of like the strap on a golf bag. The helicopter comes swooping down and guys on the ground hook up the strap and wave to 'em when it's all clear to lift. Then once the helicopter pilot gets over the platform, he slowly lowers it into place. Once all the tension's off the strap see, there's this guy waiting in a boat. He reaches up and slides the hook off."

Matthew didn't look too convinced. "Really?"

"Mister Reyes," Major said, pointing toward the lake. "Your caddy wants to know how they got the car out there."

"I heard you saying something about a helicopter," Mister Zach said. I saw him wink at Major. "And I think your theory is close. But instead of a helicopter, they get this big crane near shore. And they use it. You ever seen 'em unload a cargo ship full of cars? Those big cranes lift each car, one by one, from the bottom of a cargo ship and place 'em up on dry land. Well when they get the crane out here, they're just doing the opposite by putting a car back out on the water."

Matthew remained seated in the cart. He shook his head while hugging the steering wheel. It looked like he was forcing a smile.

"No," Ernie Banks stepped in. From his smile I knew he was in on the joke. "What they have to do is drain the lake," he said, smiling. "See, down there at the low end, they pull a big plug and all the water pours out. Just like in a bathtub. Once it's down far enough they drive the car out there and jack it up on one of those lifts. You know, the kind of lifts they have inside a garage? Well, that's what they have out there in the lake. They drive the car up on one of those jacks and lift it up to the surface. Once it's high enough," he said unable to control a giggle any longer. "They add the water back in the lake."

Matthew hopped from the cart. He wore a puzzled look on his face. Either he couldn't think of anything cute to say, or was just frustrated. All he said was, "Oh."

Matthew was no dummy. He had given up early on the idea that the car was somehow miraculously floating on the water. What was bothering him now was the mystery of how they got the car out there.

I had to admit, I wasn't so sure myself.

No one seemed to be taking his question seriously. They figured the cute question was part of the act. They were waiting for another Birdie Dance and or thumbs up from the Parm. They wanted in on the act. Funny thing was, Matthew was serious. The more outrageous the response, the more I saw his frustration grow. And I realized the dilemma. If he played it cute too often, no one would take him seriously. No matter the situation.

I thought: Where's your birdie dance now? Can't take a little friendly ribbing? Where's your magic touch of the Parm? Think you're the darling all the time and everyone loves everything that comes out of your mouth? Well, welcome to reality. Welcome to the downside of being cute. Problem is, when you're known for nothing but being cute, that's what everybody expects. When you want to be serious, you're only going to come off as trying once again to be cute.

Matthew turned his slumped shoulders and moped toward the tee. I heard him mumble. "I just wanted to know."

There was one good thing I liked about Matthew. It didn't take long for him to snap out of a grumpy mood. And soon enough, he would do just that.

And as for myself, I was witness to all kinds of things while being a caddy at the Capital City Pro-Celebrity. I was about to add a miracle to that list. Keeping my eyes and ears open to the possibilities made me realize that extraordinary incidents take place all the time. I learned about the randomness of good fortune. I once thought that miracles only happened to the neediest. What I was about to witness changed that. And no, it wasn't the thing that lifted me from that low spot while sitting on the curb waiting for my ride home. Quite the contrary. What happened next made me realize that the rich, in fact, do get richer.

11

Having quickly drained the soda can, I had thoughts of another. I eased over to the cooler. As I dug into the icy bath I heard Renee's voice. "You want a towel to wipe it off?"

I was expecting the silent treatment. I was even prepared with a loaded response if she had started an attack. I was going to bet that she hadn't moved further than fifty yards from the clubhouse. She gave me no reason to bring it up. "Thanks," I said, nodding. As a volunteer, she appeared to possess a kind demeanor. Maybe she learned something from friendly folks around her. Maybe it was the colorful apron they all wore. Whatever it was, I was hoping she would bring a little of it home. Renee's kindness towards me was enough to fall into the category of a miracle. But not compared to what happened next.

And no, the car floating atop the lake didn't suddenly roar to life, sprout pontoon hulls, and begin cutting a wake across the surface with enough speed and power to pull a pair of skiers. That would qualify as miraculous. But like I've said before, this was not a mythical, mystical, or fantasy story. And if you want a spoiler alert, don't read the next sentence. Even though that didn't happen, the Cadillac was part of the miracle.

There were plenty of witnesses. Spectators unwilling or unable to wander the course lingered near the clubhouse. They caught glimpses of the players as they passed through. While standing in one spot, a spectator could catch approach shots and finishing putts on the ninth green as well as tee shots on the par-3 tenth hole. The traveling throng that had followed us from the start clashed with the clubhouse crowd and battled for the best vantage point. The tenth tee was wrapped with the largest audience of the day. It was at least ten people deep behind the ropes. An army of spectators maneuvered toward the hole and began circling the green. A handful crammed into the shade of tall pines.

The amateurs in our group gathered at their tee. I stood next to the President. He had a grip on the rim of the upright bag. We were near the ropes, nestled by the crowd. It was a perfect view for the miracle as it unfolded.

Mister Zach was first. He bent and placed a tee in the ground.

A marshal standing nearby raised both arms and announced with a firm voice, "Quiet please." His shadow on the shaved turf looked like he was signaling a touchdown. Only difference between him and a football referee was that in one hand he held a slender sign requesting silence. The crowd quieted. That wasn't enough for the marshal. Multitudes continued to funnel past. To halt their distracting movement the marshal made another announcement. "Hold please!"

Mister Zach placed a ball on the tee. A rollercoaster ride of emotions was about to depart. Being a close observer, I felt like I was strapped in the seat next to him.

With the amusement park ride in mind, I think it will make what happened next a little more interesting if I throw in a few comparisons. For starters, patience was required to endure a long line for the rollercoaster. You passed through a turnstile and proceeded with the sweaty crowd through a maze. You snaked through the line, and depending on how you arrived, wondered what seat you might obtain on the coaster. If you were a daredevil, perhaps you hoped for the front or back seat. That's where the ride was supposed to be the most thrilling. If you were approaching the ride with some apprehension, perhaps a middle seat was best. There was unknown anticipation.

It looked to me that Mister Zach was experiencing something similar. For most of the day, the direction of his tee shots had been a mystery. He had been fighting a hook. Everything was going left. And on the tenth tee, he once again lost the battle. "Ugh," he mumbled. "Not again." The golf ball was hit well, but had too much side spin. It was on a flight path curving away from the target.

The wayward hooking golf ball headed toward the spectators. One of the marshals on the tee yelled out, "Fore left." He swung the 'Quiet Please' sign like someone directing airplanes on the tarmac.

Mister Zach cupped his hands to his mouth. "Fore!"

As the rollercoaster left the covered shelter, it made a sharp turn and started a slow climb. A greased chain, wrapped around spinning sprockets, grabbed the coaster and towed it inch by inch toward the peak. The spring-loaded safety brake ticked over metal teeth in unison with your beating heart. A fear of impeding danger.

The forward spectators in the crosshairs reacted differently. Some shaded their eyes and pointed towards the sky. It was as if they had a track on the ball in-flight and had somehow calculated they were safe. Confident in their judgment, they remained calm. Others, having heard the warning, reacted as if they were under attack of an incoming nuclear missile. They ducked and covered their heads. Several spectators seemed to remain oblivious. They stood innocently chatting quietly or sipping their drinks. They either missed the signals or were naive to any possible threat.

As Mister Zach's golf ball started its descent, it struck an outstretched branch of a pine. The sound echoed like a toy hammer repairing the roof of a wooden birdhouse. Mister Zach let out a visible sigh of relief. I'm not sure if it was due to the potential for personal injury or the possible ballooning of his score. He swiped at his brow with a forearm, staggered, and let out a, "Whew." Bounding from the bark, the ball was falling toward a greenside bunker.

At the rollercoaster summit there was a brief feeling of relief. No longer did you have to worry about the rickety ride breaking down halfway up. A misfortune like that would mean hours of supine suspension waiting to be rescued. Making it to the peak meant good old dependable gravity would take over. Nothing would stop the ride from there.

The pine tree deflection protected the crowd just as effective as a fifty foot fence. It was also fortuitous for Mister Zach. Instead of deflecting towards the parking lot, the glancing blow kept his golf ball in play.

Daredevils on the rollercoaster raised their arms. Gravity was suspended for a millisecond as the car raced towards earth. Nervous riders gripped the safety bar with white knuckles. Their stomachs rose to their throats.

I expected the deflected ball to drop into the sand bunker as soft as a marshmallow falling on a pillow. I think the crowd held the same expectations because, when the ball bounced high, spectators everywhere belted out a unified chorus of, "Whoa." "Hey." "Wow." The white orb crash landed onto something hard and ricocheted on an arc toward the putting surface. I learned later it had a fortunate meeting with a sprinkler head about the size of a banana crème pie. Upon seeing the inexplicable rebound, Mister Zach raised his arms. I think he was surrendering to logic.

Having survived the steepest dive, riders on the rollercoaster accepted the fact that the worst was over. Those with their hands raised whooped for more. Those holding tight thought about loosening their grip.

As his golf ball landed on the fringe, Mister Zach began motioning with his raised arms. It was as if he were able to push the ball through telekinesis. I was doubtful that his body English could have had such an effect, but since the flagstick was downhill from where the ball landed, it appeared to be working.

Folks sitting in folding chairs or on the ground around the green rose to their feet. Mumbles of anticipation grew.

Even Mister Zach appeared eager. I think he was holding his breath.

"Go, go," someone in the crowd urged.

The ball was picking up speed as it rolled down the hill. It began to bend toward the cup.

A voice behind me said. "Look out!"

With little steam left, the final rotation of the ball had it hovering over the lip. It seemed to linger there as if one more fortunate nudge in the form of a gust of wind seemed to push it over.

An ace.

A hole-in-one.

In unison with the disappearing ball, the crowd around the green erupted. They raised their arms and leaped. The roar traveled to the far reaches of the golf course.

Around the tee, spectators began jumping and yelling.

Mister Zach sprung the highest. "It's in!" It was like he had planned on making the shot from the beginning. "It went in!"

Those on the rollercoaster wondered if the ride was over or if there were more surprises ahead. The car made a last turn and the shed was in sight. The rickety car pulled back under the shelter making it home safely. There were smiles, hoops, hollers and requests to ride again.

Around the tee I heard, "I don't believe it."

"Oh my gosh!"

"No way."

"Nice shot, Ace," Ernie Banks said. "Maybe you could add this one as a new chapter in your next book."

"Yeah," said Zach. "I could title it, 'Divine Inspiration.'"

Out of earshot of just about everybody but me, Chip Swanson quipped out of the side of his mouth, "You gotta be kiddin' me." He was shaking his head. "Even with a hole-in-one, this guy won't break ninety."

"They don't ask how on the scorecard." Uncle Charlie smiled and patted Mister Zach on the back. "They only ask how many. You can write down a one."

It took several minutes for reality to sink in and for the crowd to settle.

The President was next on the tee. "Tough act to follow," he said.

I caught glimpses of the President. He appeared to enjoy the hole-in-one, but I got the feeling he wasn't totally impressed. He smiled, nodded, and shook hands congratulating everyone. He remained cool. He didn't go jumping around in amazement or toss his hat in the air. His reaction was simply as it should've been. It was Presidential. I guess the most powerful man in the world had seen plenty and was comfortable with chaos erupting around him. The only thing I heard him say was, "How do I follow that?" He said this to no one in particular.

It was almost impossible to calm the crowd. The President went ahead with his tee shot anyway. The ball took off on almost the same flight path as Mister Zach's. Instead of hitting the tree and bouncing off the sprinkler head, his ball was swallowed by the bunker. "Of all the rotten luck," I heard him mumble as he slid the club back into the bag.

As we walked from the tee, Mister Zach seemed to be wrapped in euphoria. "I'd rather be lucky than good," he said, hopping into the cart next to Matthew.

Before Matthew hit the gas someone in the crowd chimed in, "I guess your wife will be getting a new car?"

"No," he said. "I don't think she'll give up the one she's driving now for anything in the world."

Another boisterous voice in the crowd said, "You buying the drinks in the clubhouse?"

"You betcha," Mister Zach replied, slapping Matthew on the back. "And my caddy's getting root beer floats served in gallon buckets."

Matthew nodded and licked his lips. He gestured with a double thumbs up and then mashed the gas pedal. Halfway there I watched as he slowed down and pointed toward the car on the lake.

When they arrived at the green, Mister Zach hopped out of the cart and tiptoed toward the pin. It was as if he were sneaking up on it. As if he thought if he closed in too quickly, the ball might somehow decide to jump out. He peeked down in the hole. Once he spotted the ball resting at the bottom of the cup, he let out an exaggerated sigh of relief. He placed a hand over his heart. A few people in the crowd laughed. Mister Zach reached around the flagstick and plucked the ball from the hole. He tossed it in the air like a lucky coin. Still aware of the crowd, he pointed toward Matthew and said, "My caddy wants to know how they're going to get the car out of the water." Another smattering of laughter followed.

I heard a lady's voice, "He's so cute."

Matthew smiled and tipped his cap to the audience.

"Don't you worry, Matty," said Mister Zach. "You just worry about all those ice cream floats."

The President stood in the middle of the sand bunker waiting for Ernie Banks on the opposite side of the green. He was preparing for a chip shot. I was close enough to the unsettled crowd to hear a few lingering manic conversations.

"I can't believe you missed it," I heard a guy say, waving his hands. "It was the craziest thing ever." His buddy was carrying a beer in each hand. The guy grabbed one of the beers and kept talking. "It hit the top of that tree." He pointed toward the sky. "And came down and hit that sprinkler." He pointed at the ground. "And started rolling toward the hole." He started spinning a finger like a wheel. "And I wouldn't have believed it if I hadn't seen it with my own two eyes, but I swear to you it slammed into the pin and dropped in the cup." He bonked his own forehead with the heel of his hand.

"I heard all the screaming," his buddy said, scratching his scalp. "And saw some people jumping around. They said someone won the car. But I never saw it."

"It was wild, man." He took a sip of beer. "You wouldn't have believed it. Even if you had seen it. It was some kind of miracle."

Ernie Banks was on the green surveying a landing area for his chip shot. The conversation in the crowd continued.

"Wish they had instant replay out here."

"The only thing missing was if a bald eagle had swooped down, picked it up and carried it over to the cup and dropped it in."

"I guess the tournament will loose their shirts."

"No, no," the other voice was whispering now. "They got insurance."

"Insurance?"

"Yeah. It's the insurance company that pays up. They have *actualaries* or something like that to figure the odds. You

know, if so many people take a crack, what's the likelihood of one
going in. You know, that it will *actually* happen."

I thought about algebra class. Maybe that's the kind of
problem to solve in algebra class. I wondered if Theresa
Bellissima would know how to do the math. It would make for a
good homework assignment.

"The folks running the tournament hope someone makes a
hole-in-one," the whispered voice continued. "They pay an
insurance premium in advance. It's a lot cheaper than the cost of
the car. So they hope someone cashes in on it."

"Okay then, I bet the insurance company is cheesed off."

"Don't worry about them. They got loads of cash."

"They had to figure it was a safe bet. No way could
someone make it with all these people watching. I bet they put that
car out there in plain sight to make people nervous. They tee it up
and look at it out there and dream about driving it home. Best
distraction there could be."

"That's what makes it a miracle."

That was the last of the conversation I heard.

Ernie Banks had landed on the green and the President had
blasted from the bunker. It was my responsibility to rake the trap
smooth. To keep up, it had to be done quickly. I hopped in and
began raking. An idea came to me. I turned the rake upside down
and used the straight backside instead of the tines. I liked the
results. I thought it made the sand smooth. As I eased out, raking
my last footprint, a portly marshal approached. "You're doing it
all wrong kid," the marshal said, wagging his finger. "You got to
keep the forks down. They want to see the rake marks in the
bunkers." As I left I turned to see him enter the trap and go back
over the area. This time, with the tines down.

I lifted the bag and moved to the fringe. Everyone took a
turn putting. Everyone, that is, except Mister Zach. Ernie Banks
was the last to complete the hole. As he sank his putt, I looked up
to notice a golf cart traveling from the tee. It wasn't from the
group behind us and it wasn't quite a golf cart either.

Equipped with headlights, fenders, bumpers, grill, and
familiar hood ornament, it was customized to look like a Cadillac.
As it turned in front of the green, I noticed tailfins on the rear and

working brake lights. The midnight blue metallic paint and chrome bumpers shined in the sunlight. A man in coat and tie hopped from the passenger seat followed by a support crew outfitted with Cadillac logos. Several carried cameras and a good looking woman gripped a bouquet of balloons. "Next time," the man in the coat and tie said, slightly out of breath. "We'll have to make the players call their shot like in HORSE." The man reached inside his coat and pulled out a pair of keys. The cameras came closer. "We won't hold you up very long. We never get to do this. We wanted to catch the moment." With the floating Cadillac in the background, he smiled and handed over the keys to Mister Zach.

Although he had his detractors, Mister Zach was very much the philanthropist. Most of his work went unnoticed by the press. But what happened next was hard for me to forget.

"I've been thinking," Mister Zach said, rubbing his chin. "I do some work with some very wonderful organizations. One of them is in need of a transportation upgrade. What do you think? Could I trade in the Cadillac for a passenger van? St. Mary's Orphanage has been selling raffle tickets and hosting dinners trying to raise enough funds for a new one. I'd like to make the dream a reality for them. What do you think? Can I trade in the car for a van?"

The man in the coat and tie seemed kind of surprised. He pursed his lips and nodded. "I think that's a fine idea."

Mister Zach was pretty smart. In front of the crowd and cameras, how could the guy say no?

I know I said that the rich get richer and that I thought good fortune fell in the wrong place. That's how I felt in the beginning. But once I learned the true outcome, I had to rethink that assumption. St. Mary's Orphanage was the real beneficiary of that lucky hole-in-one. For all those that enjoyed ridiculing Mister Zach, I wondered if they continued to make the same mistake too.

12

When it came to caddying for the President, most of the time was spent in one of two modes; either hurry-up or wait. The hurry-up part was basically any time we moved from point A to point B. And yes, the hurry-up mode was directly related to the keep up rule of being a caddy. Some times there were departures from a tee down a swath of mowed turf that felt like a catwalk. Other times we covered the ground of vast fairways like a beach invasion. While on the move, my stride jostled the iron clubs causing them to chatter. The ticking noise was constant as a stopwatch. Often I had to reach back and stuff the dangling towel between the offending utensils. When we left putting greens, it was usually through roped off paths that felt like tunnels. Lining each side were cheering fans waiting for a close-up encounter. Some kids held out a hand hoping someone would slap them five. The hurry-up mode used up a lot of muscle power. For that reason, I started to look forward to the wait mode.

It was a chance to catch my breath and unload the bag. My shoulders thanked me for that. Sometimes the wait was short. On the tees, in the fairways, around hazards, and on the putting greens, a few sweet minutes were spent waiting for other players to execute their shots. Sometimes the wait stretched longer. Impromptu performances from celebrities, searches for lost balls, penalty strokes, and general slow play. Waiting gave my legs and shoulders a rest, but not my brain.

No matter which mode, I stuck near the President. And when it came to learning new things, the mode didn't seem to matter either. I learned during both hurry-up and wait. Most of the things had to do with being a better caddy. But I also learned a few things about myself.

We came to a halt in the twelfth fairway. The group ahead was searching for a lost ball. The President slid over to Uncle Charlie and interrogated him for a few more swing pointers. Not interested in their conversation, I eased the bag off my shoulder and stood in the first cut of rough. Matthew loitered near his cart with a towel wrapped around his neck. Mister Zach stood next to his ball in the fairway. Chip Swanson stood next to the cart. I heard him saying, "They build a bridge and drive it out there. Then they tear down the bridge. When the tournament's over, they rebuild the bridge and drive back off. Pretty simple really."

I was growing tired of the floating car mystery. I was more interested in catching another glimpse of Theresa Bellissima. I searched nearby faces in the crowd but came up empty.

Something did catch my eye. It touched me and got me thinking. And the thinking led to another important discovery.

It was a dad talking to whom I assumed was his son. "This is the first time I've ever seen a President in person," said the hushed voice of the father, squatting near the ropes like a catcher relaying signals. He instructed the boy at eye-level. "This is your first time too." A worn bucket hat with a fishing reel logo covered his wooly hair. It looked as if he had kept a relaxed Saturday morning ritual of skipping a shave. There were moth holes in his grey unbuttoned sweater.

The boy, about ten years old, wore a short sleeve dress shirt and baseball cap. Athletic socks sagged around his ankles. He pressed his flat hand against the bill of his cap. I couldn't tell if he was shading the sun or saluting the President.

Bumble Bee Bakery tickets fluttered on both their belt loops.

"I've never been to Washington D.C. or anywhere like that," the dad said, resting a plump hand on the shoulder of the boy. He pointed with the other hand. "But look right there. Right there is the President of the United States."

"That's him alright." The boy smiled and nodded. He was a younger version of his dad, even gesturing with the same mannerisms. "His picture's on the wall at school. I walk by it everyday."

"Joey, Joey," the dad said, turning away from the fairway. "Get over here." He motioned with the free hand.

Swinging upside down on a branch behind them was a young boy. "Hey Dad," a giggling Joey pleaded. "Look at me." His assault on the innocent trunk and smooth bark was as natural as if it were monkey bars on the playground. He had both legs looped over a limb and was hanging upside down with his arms crossed over his chest. "I'm a bat," he declared, slightly swaying while trying to hold the pose. "Just like a vampire."

"That's good, that's good, Joey," his dad nodded. "Now come down." He motioned with a hand. "Get over here, this is the reason we're here."

Joey remained upside down in the tree.

"Get down from there now."

"You gotta say the magic word," Joey said still frozen in the pose.

"Now," his dad responded through clenched teeth.

Joey grabbed the branch and somersaulted from the limb. Evidently, the magic word was, 'Now.'

"I've waited my whole life for something like this," the dad said, corralling Joey by the shoulders. "And here you are, getting to see a real, living, breathing President."

Joey reached for the yellow rope and began shaking it. His fingernails were crammed with dirt and the front of his T-shirt was stained with grape Sno-cone juice.

"Sit still Joey," the dad said, pulling Joey out of reach of the dangling barrier. "See that man out there?" He pointed to the fairway. "That's the President. It's the first time in my life to see a President. And look how old I am. It's your first time too. And look how young you are. I hope you'll get to see a bunch more by the time you're old as me."

The older son nodded.

Joey reached out, grabbed the rope again, and started shaking.

I had to smile. I wasn't even sure if they knew I was watching or could hear what they were saying. I doubted they would even care if I could.

It reminded me of my dad. It stirred something in me. Several years before, he had brought Matthew and me to this same tournament. We didn't get to see a President then, but we did see Johnny Bench. It reminded me of the times we had together and how much I missed him.

Seeing the boys with their dad triggered something. A revelation. A discovery. Sure, there was no doubt that I missed my dad. But until then, I hadn't realized how much I had missed his encouragement. He often challenged me. I would do anything to seek his approval and never turned down a challenge. I once climbed a ten meter diving platform and jumped into the deep end of a swimming pool to prove to him that I was brave enough to do it. I remembered gripping the chrome railing with wet hands. Steps on the ladder were covered with something similar to sandpaper. The dizzying height. Summoning the courage to step off the perilous edge. Eyes closed. The wind whistling in my ears as I plunged. The surface slapping at the soles of my feet. Half-scared out of my wits. I climbed out of the pool and received a grin and a wink of approval. "I didn't think you could do it," my dad said. I'd do anything for those grins and winks.

What I had with my dad wasn't that much different from what others had. I saw the two boys with their father looking at the President. I realized that most sons, at some level, seek the approval of their father. And maybe that was a big reason for missing my dad. I hadn't realized it before, but it was part of the discovery. I would never again be able to earn one of those smiling winks. For me, his approval and recognition would have to be assumed. Or, it would have to come from somewhere else.

That was a pretty big breakthrough. If the leap from the ten meter platform story fell short, there were more examples. Standing there waiting for the golf course to clear, I thought of another one.

The memory evoked an even deeper universal truth. That was, that if a father's approval was important to a son, there was a shortcut. Follow in your father's footsteps. It was a surefire way to connect. For me, that meant signing up for peewee football. I'm sure it was part of my motivation. My dad had played football as a boy and through high school. When I was too young to play, he coached a peewee football team. I spent years on the sidelines waiting until I was old enough. Reaching a certain age was only half the hurdle. To be eligible to play, I had to have also reached a certain weight. I remember the weigh-in. It was held at a nearby park on a Saturday morning. On the eve of the weigh-in, a neighbor across the street instructed me to request homemade biscuits for breakfast. He said it would improve my chances of making the weight. I asked my mom and she convinced me that he was only kidding. I told her that homemade biscuits still sounded good for breakfast. We woke up early. I had homemade biscuits. I felt old enough and heavy enough to ride in the front seat next to my dad. I even joked, "Maybe I should put some rocks in my pockets." He smiled and told me not to worry about it. I stood in line with the other kids. We made our way toward the scales. I handed in my signed permission slip and stepped up. The hand swept across the dial and teetered just above the recommended level. I had proven myself worthy of football.

I'm not sure why I included this part about the weigh-in. I guess it was like some kind of modern-day rite of passage. Kind of like the first time a caveman took out his son to throw spears at mastodons. It wasn't until two years later that my dad was actually a coach of my team. But I guess it's a good reminder of why I took up football in the first place. I wanted to follow in his footsteps. I wanted to connect.

I was twelve years old when my dad coached my team. That meant he was nearby to watch my every move. If something good happened, he wouldn't miss it. And maybe that was the lucky part. He was there to see the greatest play in my football career.

I didn't score a touchdown or recover a fumble in front of a cheering crowd. I wasn't even wearing a game-day jersey. The greatest football play in my career happened during a routine scrimmage. I was on the defensive line. I was matched up against a kid that was both taller and had more than a few pounds on me. That usually meant a lot in football. But on this day, it didn't seem to matter much. For some reason, I was feeling stronger. I was feeling faster. I was feeling smarter. I was feeling bigger. It was like I was able to predict when the ball was going to be snapped. I was beating the big kid to the punch. He couldn't stop me. His job was to keep me from invading the offensive front, yet I was consistently breaking through. I had found a weak spot, a gap that was easy to penetrate. It was just to the side of him. It made complete sense to me. Why line directly in front of someone if your ultimate goal was to get around them? I took advantage of the weak spot. I had found it and made the opponent look foolish because of it. Each time, just as the ball was snapped, a burst of energy sprang me through the gap.

My success was not going unnoticed. I took occasional glances in my dad's direction. He was coaching the offense and was hardly in a position to urge me on. But, he was giving me an occasional glancing grin and nod of the head. These gestures were mild compared to what I got for the greatest football play ever.

The quarterback on our team was what could be classified as a prima donna. Yes, he was probably the best athlete on the team. And yes, he was the only one capable of handling each snap of the football and distributing it to the right player by either handing it off or passing it down the field. He was also smart enough to remember the plays, call them in the huddle, remember the snap count, and make sure everyone was in the right place at the right time. But he wasn't very tough. He was known to actually shed tears when things didn't go his way. Anyone balling over anything, especially in sports, was easily labeled a poor sport or a crybaby. I think he was also allergic to grass and mud stains. He'd do anything to avoid them. He would duck and cover just before being tackled or try to escape contact by running out of bounds. His dad told him it was the smart thing to do. His teammates thought differently.

Our quarterback was overconfident. You know, the hot dog kid, the one that worried about appearance and always had a clean uniform. He wore expensive cleats. He ran his taped fingers through his blond highlighted hair each time he took off his helmet. What kind of guy would sit in a beauty parlor and allow someone to put dye in their hair? And what was with the tape on the fingers? And for that much, what about the red, white and blue wristbands? Sweat bands in wintertime? He was also too cool to remember anybody's name on the team. He called everybody dude. He wore a pukka shell necklace. A real pretty boy. And did I mention he whimpered when things didn't go his way?

His jersey number couldn't be the standard quarterback number twelve. I think he even whined when first told his choice of number wasn't available. The team had to make a special order. His dad agree to pay the extra cost because he believed there was no better jersey number for his son than the number one.

His dad was probably a big part of the problem. He was an overbearing sight on the sidelines. All the other parents grew tired of the constant boasting about his son's skills and the flood of future scholarship offers that would come his way. It was rumored that his father had kept him back in school so that he would be the oldest and most experienced on the field. Problem for our quarterback, most everyone on our team knew his heart wasn't really into it. As much as his father was pushing him to become a great quarterback, the kid lacked some level of desire. He didn't yearn for greatness on the same level as his dad.

So, back to the greatest football play of my career. I was having a good day whipping the bigger kid across the line and busting through the gaps in the line of scrimmage. With all this in mind, I began to narrow my aim on the prima donna quarterback. I hungered to crash into him with ferocity. I wanted to make him cry. We were well into the practice when the time came. The ball was snapped. I shot the gap easily escaping the blocking attempt of the big kid. I found myself in the offensive backfield.

The prima donna was dropping back to throw a pass. I charged like a bull. With all the force I had, I lowered my head and drove my helmet into his chest. It was like I was trying to run right through the guy. The impact stung. My spine stiffened and my ears rang. The whistle blew. I opened my eyes to see the blue sky. Next to me on the ground I heard a moan. The quarterback was squirming on the ground. I rose to my knees. Like a spoiled kindergartner, the quarterback started to rock and cry.

I had conquered a foe. The violent attack and overpowering victory lifted me. I felt mighty. Since the beginning of time, certain men understood the feeling of being conquerors. At that point, I shared those feelings.

It was something my dad seemed to understand. I looked over to him and saw the look on his face. His smiling eyes were large and peered directly into my own. He pursed his smiling lips and nodded in my direction. He then gave me a wink. I'm not sure if anyone else saw the exchange, but it was a golden moment. My dad didn't have to parade along the sidelines bragging. He never cheered my name. He never boasted to other parents. He never made a public spectacle of himself or me. As the quarterback rolled on the ground crying my dad gave me a wink and a smile. It was worth more than any Olympic medal, any silver cup, any trophy, or any blue ribbon ever handed out in any athletic event ever held.

So, if you're wondering what all this talk about football has to do with being a caddy, let me explain. You see, it was there, while caddying for the President and listening to that dad with his two sons that I had learned something. For the first time, I was reminded that I would never have another chance to look over to my dad. There would be no more winks. There would be no more challenges to jump from the high dive. There would be no more smiles. No more nods of recognition. No more encouraging gestures for a job well done. No more chances to make a connection. I had never thought about it before. I knew I missed him, but I couldn't completely explain why. It was those smiles and winks. They would no longer be available as rewards.

If I could, I would gladly go up against the entire front line of the Pittsburgh Steelers to win another.

13

This wasn't much of a mystery story. There were no built in crimes to be solved or bank robbers to nab. No whodunit. No ticking bombs to be defused. No Professor Plum in the Billiard Room with a candlestick. The least mysterious bunch during the day was the Secret Service. From what I could see, there wasn't much secret about them. The one agent standing nearby most of the day was easy to spot. His suit and tie wasn't exactly camouflage mode, but he tried to maintain a clandestine impression. He often pressed at the disc in his ear and mumbled into his cufflinks. When the President's tee shot veered right of the playing grounds on the thirteenth hole, several other agents scrambled to the spot. The ball came to rest in shin-high grass and eager spectators circled like a pack of hungry wolves. One of the agents had binoculars lifted to his eyes and aimed at a nearby high-rise apartment building. He scanned every window and terrace. A few late-arriving marshals stretched their arms to circle the President's golf ball. One of the marshals tired to joke with an agent, "The way the President's spraying it around, I think you guys should be out here protecting the crowd from him." The agents remained stone-faced. Outside a chain link fence on the opposite side of the fairway, a few uniformed police officers were parked along the graveled shoulder of the road. They were leaning against their motorcycles. There were no mysteries about security.

The show of force seemed to work. Throughout the day, there were only two incidents that came close to posing any type of threat. Both of them miniscule. No unsolved mysteries. Open and shut cases. Slam dunks. Barely a blip on the radar screen.

The first one came as we strolled past a crowd on the fourth hole. A faceless dissident that probably drew courage from too many beers tossed a snide remark toward the President. Accustomed to taunts, the President smiled, raised a hand, and waved. His response was the same as if someone had called out something supportive. The second threat from the crowd came at the top of the President's backswing on the eighth hole. That time, an infant squealed. The disruption caused the President to shank a seven-iron. But he responded the same. He smiled, raised a hand, and waved.

The heightened security did something for me. It reminded me of the importance of the man I was working for. That was no mystery.

That word, extraordinary, came to mind again. The security detail was providing an extraordinary level of protection. I wanted to match that level. Earlier, I wondered why. But now, maybe that mystery was solved. Maybe I was hoping for a nod, a smile, a wink, a thank you from the President for a job well done. Maybe I was seeking something simple as that. A bit of recognition. But the more I thought about it, the more I had a feeling that I wouldn't be getting such prizes from the President. He was, after all, the President. And, he had battalions of troops falling all over themselves for his approval.

And the President, he wasn't much of a mystery either. He didn't appear to seek approval from anyone. I got the feeling that he had all the recognition he could handle. It was commonplace. As we traveled around the golf course, spectators showered him with appreciation. We approached waiting crowds and they began to applaud. It wasn't the raucous clamoring for a movie star. There were no resounding chants for sports figures. No cheers. No yells. There was just a considerate smattering. A calm greeting. A courtesy extended. A single person usually lit the fuse. The initiator usually made the person standing next to him or her feel obligated to join. It grew like a chain reaction. The round of applause followed us. It started ahead of us, grew louder on arrival, and then faded as we passed. The President didn't even have to hit a good golf shot. I got the feeling most of the people in the crowd weren't following his score. The ovation was gratitude.

It reminded me that the job of being the President's caddy was a reward in itself. I had been told that many times before and it should've sunk in. The job was a privilege. It was an honor that I knew I hadn't really earned. If not for Uncle Charlie I would have been just another bystander outside the ropes. And I guess that was another discovery. I figured that sometimes you get rewarded for things you really don't deserve. Maybe that made up for the times when you got overlooked.

In a sense, I was striving for extraordinary on Uncle Charlie's behalf. He stuck his neck out for me, and I wanted to do my best for him.

And that wasn't so easy when there were so many distractions. And if someone was looking for a mystery in this story, maybe there was something.

Theresa Bellissima was a mystery. She was also a distraction. I spotted her lingering by the ropes. I wanted to go over and talk, but my duty required me to stay close to the President. She waved in my direction. I nodded and smiled.

As she waved, the wide strap of Theresa Bellissima's sundress slipped off her opposite shoulder. It curled and dangled around her bare shoulder. Okay, it wasn't totally bare. There was a lacy pink bra strap. It clung tightly to her skin. The sagging collar didn't drop far enough to expose much more. But what I saw was enough to grab my attention. She reached over and casually tugged the collar back in place. But it was too late. I got an eye full. Then I began to wonder. Why had she left it dangling for so long? Was I supposed to see something? Was it her way of grabbing me by the shoulders and shaking me until I paid attention? If so, it worked. Or, was I not supposed to look? Was she at first unaware of the bared bra strap? Was she actually feeling embarrassed? Was it some kind of wardrobe malfunction? Had I in fact stolen a glimpse of unmentionables? Either way, I couldn't undo it. I had seen what I had seen. The image was seared in my brain. Lacy lingerie tended to do that. The real mystery for me was trying to figure out if the bare skin was flaunted for my benefit or a simple mishap.

Maybe this unsolved case was better left for another story. Maybe I should highlight or flag these paragraphs to reread for some possible editing. Maybe even leave it out completely. In that case, when my mom or Megan read this, they won't think I'm a complete pervert. Then again, Matthew might like to read these parts. He would probably like it. If not now, in a few years.

"Who you waving to?"

The question startled me. I turned to notice Major. Uncle Charlie's bag was draped over his shoulder. The distraction allowed him to sneak up.

"A girl from school," I said. I was glad it was Major. I looked around to see the President chewing the fat with Uncle Charlie. I'm glad the President didn't catch me off guard. The Secret Service agents probably weren't too impressed that I could be so easily distracted by a pretty face.

Major stood the bag on the ground. "She's cute."

"Yeah." I wanted to change the subject. "Back there on the tee," I motioned with a head nod. "What were you looking at?"

"Checking the wind."

"You can see the wind?"

"Sure. See the top of that tree. See how it moves. Look at the flagstick. Check out the ripples on the lake. All those things give clues. The direction. How strong it might be. It might even swirl."

"That why you toss the grass?"

"I just kind of let the blades go and see which way they fall."

"I have to admit," I said. "Being a caddy is not as easy as I thought." It wasn't much of a confession. I had argued the same point with Renee for weeks. But it was something I wanted Major to hear from me.

"If it were easy," Major said, "it wouldn't be as rewarding." After a few seconds, he added, "The secret is to make it look easy. And never give up."

"I don't plan on giving up," I said. "I'm out here today trying to get better."

"Giving up comes easy to some people. This one guy I know gave up golf altogether. He was a great player, but could never shoot lower than 72. He got close many times, but could never go lower. Something always went wrong. Early or late. If he shot 32 on the front, he would pair it with a 40. When it came down to the last hole, he could never finish it. Once all he needed was a double bogey, and wouldn't you know it, he made a triple. It was enough for him to give up completely. That's when he became a caddy."

The President approached. He grabbed the rim of the bag and shook it. He examined the contents. He lifted a club, took hold of the grip, and took a practice swing. I reached down and grabbed a handful of grass. I held it high in the air and then let it go. I felt like a downfield wide receiver waving a hand above my head hoping to catch the attention of the scrambling quarterback. As the grass clippings drifted to earth, I tried to interpret the wind. I don't think the President saw any of it. I was wide open but he never threw me the ball. Never even saw me. He never asked for my advice. He never asked for anything. Not even a club. Each time, he reached into his own bag and retrieved the club he wanted. No mystery there. *Keep trying,* I thought. Keep waving that hand over your head. Maybe he'll notice I'm open. Maybe he'll toss me something before it's over.

14

"Look out for snakes," Chip Swanson said as we walked together from the next tee. "I hate snakes."

The President had once again sent his tee shot beyond the boundaries. This time, to the right. There was no need for yellow rope to hold back spectators. The thick wooded area was so inhospitable to mankind, the crowds were not allowed anywhere near the area.

"Snakes?"

"Yeah, I know a guy was bit by a water moccasin in there."

"Water moccasin?"

"Yeah, there's a creek running along the same direction as the fairway."

"Creek?" The vegetation screened everything like a vine-covered wall.

"Yeah," Chip Swanson said. "You won't catch me going in there. Automatic lost ball for me. I hate snakes." He picked up his pace and veered toward the center of the fairway.

It was at this point that I realized the day had a safari feel to it.

The President had got ahead of me. I hurried to keep up. By the time he made it to the edge of the thicket, I was standing next to him. A lone marshal, standing on the edge of darkness, greeted us. "I saw where it went in, sir." He was wearing a pith helmet. "It was right in this direction." He turned and pointed.

I eased the bag off my shoulder. The marshal took a step into the jungle. The President remained in the clearing.

My Language Arts teacher said that I had a healthy imagination. She encouraged me to put it to use in my story. Like the cheering crowd for the inside-the-park home run, the Kool-Aid man busting through the woods, and the roller coaster ride. They were examples of where and when I let my mind take a vacation. That's what happened over hours of being a caddy. As a matter of fact, the Big Goof probably occurred because my mind wandered when it shouldn't have. But I'll get to that soon enough. As I stood outside that jungle, I could think of nothing but a safari. I was about to actually shed some blood. So it wasn't such a farfetched idea.

"I can see it," the marshal wearing the pith helmet said. "It's on the other side of the creek, tangled up in a brier patch."

Maybe my healthy imagination came from watching too many movies. I liked to drink in the vivid scenes. I liked to figure out what they meant. I liked to put myself there. So as the day of caddying drug out, I couldn't help but think about a jungle safari. The expedition was grueling and taking a toll.

"It's mine alright," the President said, stepping far enough away from safety to peer through the brush. "I can see enough of it to identify it." He turned and headed back toward the fairway.

"You want me to get it, sir?" Here was my chance, I thought. This was the perfect opportunity for me to provide some extraordinary service. "I can get it for you."

I didn't need to wait for his response. I took a step over the creek. I was thinking of the safari. Maybe this tale had elements to make it a jungle safari story—I was nothing—one of the local natives recruited to carry a pack through the harsh terrain—forced servitude—mules, oxen, even elephants loaded with packs—I heard elephants had a long memory—toting the golf bag, I was a beast of burden—hauling the essential, rudimentary, provisions—oppressive heat wringing the sweat from my pores, suffocating humidity, laden branches covered with moss and creeping vines—stagnant puddles harboring mosquitoes—mysterious pockets of shade—clouds of gnats orbiting my skull—leeches—quick sand—slashing through choking growth, clinging vines, sinewy seedlings, leafs the size of hubcaps—chirping, whistling, squawking exotic birds—howling monkeys, laughing hyenas, roaring lions—all mocking me—creeping spiders, centipedes with a thousand waving legs—a python balled up in a branch—waiting to pounce on me—malaria, typhoid, dengue fever—waiting to infect me—swinging machete, tromping through the muck, decaying logs, rotting piles of brush—termite mounds, swarms of killer bees, blood-sucking mosquitoes, ferocious flies, venomous vipers, stinging scorpions—hacking through the growth so that those following will have it easier—carrying the load to make their trip easier—you are not in charge—you are only needed for your strong legs and back—if you happen to drop from exhaustion, we have someone waiting and willing to pick up the load—you are expendable—did I mention the heat?

"Hey, Chuck," I heard the President's voice back in the fairway. I knew immediately he wasn't talking to me. His voice was raised and seemed to be directed away from me. "This a lateral hazard?"

Back in civilization, I heard Uncle Charlie's voice but couldn't really pick up his response.

Iron clubs rattled in the bag. I figured the President was near enough to hear me. Since he hadn't answered the first time, I tried again. This time, a little louder. "You want me to pick up your ball, sir?"

"Don't worry about it," he said after a few seconds. It was like he had forgotten I was attempting the rescue. "I'm going to take a drop."

That wasn't enough to make me give up. A good caddy, I thought, would return with any lost ball within reach. So I hunched over to fetch it. I realized how the President had identified the ball. Around the number there was a blue circle made with a magic marker. If anyone had asked me before being his caddy, I would have assumed the President's golf ball would have more elaborate markings or perhaps a nickname, like 'The Prez' stamped on it. Or even a profile of the White House or an official seal of the office. But that was not the case. The President played golf balls right off the shelf, just like you and me. And I have to admit, if there was something that actually gained my respect and admiration, it was that fact alone. He wasn't royalty. No one had to bow to him.

And as for snatching the ball from the brush, that proved trickier than I first thought. It cost me some blood. No, I didn't get bitten by a water moccasin. And no, I didn't have to fight off a souvenir seeker. It was simpler than that. I was assaulted by a thorn.

I thought back to that jungle safari. The golf ball was now an archeological relic. It was in sight, and I was determined to return with it.

Thorny branches engulfed the ball. Near the base of a tree, woody vines curled around gnarly roots. I wondered if poison ivy lurked nearby. I dreaded any chance encounter with its insidious sap that would wreak havoc within hours and sprout itchy blisters that would linger for days. I wondered what possible creatures crept underneath the growth waiting to strike. It was the perfect spot for a covered pit with a bed of pointed spikes. A layer of decaying leaves blanketed the path. If I had to pick a spot to dig for earthworms, I believe I could've filled a paper cup within a few minutes, enough to keep a hook baited for a whole afternoon. An aluminum soda can, with its red logo sun-faded to pink, was half-buried in the muck. Forget about those things. Grab the ball.

I bent and grabbed the prize. As I started back out of the bramble, a thorn ripped into the underside of my right forearm. Once the nerves sent the pain message to my brain, my reaction was to pull away faster. That was a mistake. The razor-sharp point ripped deeper, slashing into my skin. I clutched the ball tighter. I lifted the underside of my arm to inspect the wound. Blood trickled from the red streak. I hopped over the creek and escaped. The President was sliding a club back into the standing bag. I held up the ball. "Got it, sir."

"Thanks, son," he said. After I dropped it into his open palm, he stuffed it in his pocket and started walking down the fairway. He didn't notice the injury.

I was a fool to think I could go into the jungle and return unscathed. I was lured by the promise of treasure and the possible reward for its return. I ignored the dangerous thorns. I should've known better or been more cautious. As I hurried my pace to keep up, I used the caddy bib as a dressing and dabbed at the bloody streak. A few minutes later I noticed the resulting stain smeared across the tournament logo. It was my red badge of courage. To be a caddy, I was willing to sacrifice my lifeblood. To finish the loop, a little determination was needed. So I mustered some up, loaded it across my shoulder, and carried on.

I was a good pack mule on this safari. Even through danger. Even through bloodshed. I was keeping up. I was following that rule. I stood nearby the President. But what happened on the next hole, when I failed to follow the rule about keeping my mouth shut, the reaction was worse than a punch in the nose. No, it wasn't the Big Goof, but it was a dire omen that things were headed in the wrong direction.

15

Double Trouble was the signature hole at Spring House Country Club. It was so nicknamed for a pair of challenges. First of these difficulties was a sloping fairway that required a drive packed with both distance and accuracy. There was no room for error. A deep thicket of trees, mostly pines straight as cellblock bars, lined both sides of the fairway. At best, the tall conifers jailed errant tee shots and then smothered them in a blanket of pine straw. At worst, tee shots ricocheted into a water hazard or out-of-bounds. Adding a stroke and re-teeing was commonplace. If fortunate enough to avoid the first round of trouble, a precise long-iron was needed from the fairway to avoid a lake that wrapped around an elevated green. It took precision and plenty of steam to keep the approach shot above the watery graveyard. The circle of shame, a designated area to drop a ball back into play, had to be moved daily due to the profuse amount of divots. Even when members happened to arrive on or near the green with the best two shots of the round, to earn a par they were still required to muster all their putting skills to execute no more than two strokes on an undulating green. A portrait of Double Trouble adorned the cover of the scorecard. Several local golf magazines named it the toughest hole in the city.

What happened on the demanding hole left me thinking that Double Trouble was probably a good nickname for me as well. Like I said, what happened next wasn't the Big Goof, but it was a sign that things were heading in the wrong direction.

The weary gallery grew impatient. In the fairway ahead, a marshal signaled to halt. An ongoing search for a lost ball meant a red light for anyone back on the tee hoping to proceed. I heard a voice in the crowd, "I've been waiting all day to see how they're gonna handle this hole." There were a handful of spectators that would've been better off at a NASCAR event. They were like the fans up in the grandstand with an appetite for the crunching of sheet metal, the smoking of braking tires, and the bursting of flames from a ten car pileup.

Ernie Banks lingered near the ropes. "It's no problem," I heard him saying. The crowd around him appeared friendly. Always smiling, he held a pen and was signing a page of an opened program. "When someone asks me for an autograph, I take it as a compliment. When someone asks, it's almost like a reward. It doesn't take me two seconds." He handed back a cap and grabbed a baseball trading card. "It doesn't cost me anything. I think I owe it to the fans. They're the ones that paid my salary. They're the reason advertisers pay the big bucks. There's nobody more important than fans." He stood next to a couple of kids wearing Chicago Cubs caps. Someone snapped a photo. "Besides," he continued, "I just like people. And if they recognize me and mention they liked the way I played, well that just adds a little extra. It's like they're saying, hey, you did a good job out there. I noticed it, and I want to say hello, shake your hand, and have you sign your name."

The President spent the time delay conversing with Uncle Charlie. I listened to Ernie Banks dispensing his philosophy to the crowd and couldn't help but compare him with the President. I couldn't think of a single time the President had stopped and signed autographs. It wasn't because no one had failed ask. There were plenty of people waving programs and hats across the ropes. The few times he acknowledged their request, he half-waved and calmly remarked, "At the end of the round." He dished out the same careful response each time. "Catch me at the end of the round. I'll be glad to sign when we get through."

I guess I can't blame him for postponing. Maybe he didn't want to loose concentration on his golf game. Or better yet, maybe it was a matter of national security. His signature had clout. He was once the most powerful man in the free world. With a stroke of his pen, he could approve or veto laws. The very same signature endorsed treaties and pacts with nations and republics. No doubt it was a powerful thing and held some value. So, I really didn't think much of the fact when he deferred requests to sign a cap or program. I understood and even empathized. Maybe I had no right to question his motives. Like when he called me Farmer.

When Uncle Charlie first asked if I wanted to caddy for the President, I didn't think much of it. But within days, I realized that the world was possibly being laid at my doorstep. I would meet the President of the United States. I would do a good job. We would become close friends. If I ever needed anything in the future, I could just pick up the phone and give my old pal the President a jingle to see if he could pull a few strings in my favor. As I got closer to the date, I began to realize that it was some pretty wishful thinking, almost juvenile. But I can't deny that it crossed my mind.

As we waited, I started to think about what was really possible. What did I want to get from being a caddy for the President? I already decided it wasn't fame or fortune. I tended to shy from the cameras. I knew what few dollars I might receive would be less than what I could make mowing lawns. So what was it? Was I still thinking about a future job with Uncle Charlie? He was anything but lukewarm to that idea. Maybe it was something as simple as someone saying 'nice job.' Maybe I was looking for a simple pat on the back. A wink or a nod. A little something for the effort. Acknowledgement. I figured out early that it probably wasn't going to come from the President. That would be asking too much from a man that was constantly surrounded by people falling all over themselves to get his attention. And I was beginning to learn that I couldn't compete with world-class service. But maybe someone somewhere would give me what I was looking for.

As we faced Double Trouble, these things were running around in my head. Again, a name I could give myself soon enough.

There's an old piece of advice that goes something like, 'It's better to leave some things unsaid.' Whoever came up with the caddy rule, 'Keep your mouth shut,' must've had that in mind. So far, if I had to make an honest assessment, I hadn't really done a perfect job of following that rule. Throughout the round, after the President executed something noteworthy, I occasionally nodded and commented, "Good shot, sir." Each of those remarks seemed to be received warmly by the President with his own nod and smile. But like all rules, if pushed too far, I would soon realize there was a price to pay.

The President hammered a nice drive that found the fairway. It was a perfect start to the first leg of Double Trouble. As he handed back the driver, I may have even offered him a nod and said, "Nice drive, sir." Or did I keep quiet? I can't remember. Now that I think about it, maybe he slid the club back into the bag himself. I guess it really didn't matter.

What I do remember was the crowd. They were at least five deep lining the fairway left of the tee. They applauded as we passed. Some of their shins were stained. Matthew had sped past in the cart. When he hit a pothole, a mud puddle spewed its contents toward the line of spectators. Matthew neither slowed nor turned around to apologize. The crowd didn't seem upset or insulted. A few of them were smiling. I heard laughing. I watched as an older woman wiped her leg with a napkin. She was smiling. I heard her say to someone nearby, "He's so cute in that cart." They loved Matthew no matter what.

In the fairway, Ernie Banks was furthest from the green. He was to play first. I stood next to the President. We were close enough to hear Chip Swanson doling out instructions. "I normally try to cozy up a little 6-iron cut shot to this postage stamp." He used the standing bag like a podium as he addressed Ernie Banks. They both took occasional glances at the golf ball. The top of it was exposed in the short rough. Chip Swanson pointed to the sky and threw around the fancy language. "But the lie you've got looks a little juicy. I'd take a 5-iron, play it back in my stance and catch it flush with a three-quarter swing. Let it carry the hazard and chase up the gap with enough speed to get pin high." If that weren't enough, he added more as Ernie Banks stood over the ball. "We got a hook lie. The hay will probably catch the heel and turn the toe over a bit, so aim a little right."

Once again, I needed a dictionary, a thesaurus, or a code book to decipher his message. I understood the part about aiming right, but I had no idea for what reason. Water was there. And as for the rest of it, I started to understand why Chip Swanson made a good caddy. His words were colorful. If by chance he didn't know what he was talking about, his instructions were certainly packed with confidence and delivered with enough authority that anyone would have to believe he held some superior advantage. He sounded good. Chip Swanson was a great promoter. Probably as good as Don King. And as State Champion, he was credible. He was popular. Probably on the same level as the Bumble Bee Baker.

Now that I look back on it, maybe I was trying to be too much like Chip Swanson. It was a mistake to think I could use the fancy language. To impress with words. Have a nose for prose. I was about to learn the hard way that saying too much at the wrong time would get you in trouble. What I should have done, was just tried to be more like myself. And kept my mouth shut.

Ernie Banks made a shot that landed safely on the green. I followed the President to his waiting ball in the fairway. The bag began to feel like a stack of bricks that I was hauling for a mason. I didn't quite have the skills to drop in a keystone or stack them plum for a foundation, but my labor was needed nonetheless to erect a building. I stood the bag next to the President. He pulled out a 6-iron.

There was no time for me to toss blades of grass in the air. There was no time to make sure the President was properly aimed at the target. No time for any flowery instructions from a caddy. I barely had enough time to pull the bag away and hold still. The President let loose his swing.

It was less than perfect. The result was disastrous. A huge divot was torn into the sod. A pair of ducks rose from the water surface. A few gasps were released from the crowd. The

President's golf ball, requiring all the fuel it could hold to fly over the water, left the launch pad with a tank that was half full.

It plopped into the water.

I said something. I wanted to eat the words as soon as they passed my lips. I made the mistake of trying to sound good. I tried to deliver a message with confidence like Chip Swanson. What was stirring around in my head and what I wanted to say was, "I'm paying attention, sir. Trying to do a good job. I was watching the whole time. From the take off, and as it flew through the air, I kept my eye on the ball. As it started falling from its summit, I tracked its direction hoping for a safe landing. I'm just trying to do my best. I'm just the messenger, sir. So, don't shoot the messenger. But I feel it is part of my duties to pass along some unfortunate news. I'm sorry to inform you, sir. But that shot that looked so wonderful flying through the air has come up short. It has splashed down in the middle of the lake. Again, I'm sorry sir that it ended up this way. And I'm sorry to be the one breaking such ill-fated news. I hope you understand. I'm just trying to do a good job."

That's the thoughts that were swimming around in my brain. And that's what I wanted to say to the President. But that's not exactly what came out of my mouth.

Right after the President's tee shot splashed down I said, "Looks like that one landed in the water, sir." I shaded my eyes and looked up at the President.

His jaws were locked tight as a safe. With a stranglehold on the grip, he lifted the club as if he were about to drive a railroad spike. Instead, he lowered it to a horizontal position. He then bared his teeth. Through his tight lips, he grumbled, "I know it, son." His voice was steely, like that of Commander-in-Chief. The glare was capable of intimidating a rogue despot.

He handed me the club, turned away, and marched toward the drop area. I followed close behind. I had failed to keep my mouth shut. His rough response echoed in my head, "I know it, son." The glare cut through my guts. The last thing he wanted to hear from anybody, even his caddy, was a reminder of the obvious. Especially if the obvious was disastrous. I was trying to be helpful. I didn't mean for the words to come off like a wisecrack. But I guess the President caught it that way. I felt even worse for some reason, when he called me, 'Son.' I thanked goodness for his restraint. He probably wanted to let loose with a few curse words aimed in my direction. I almost wished he would've called me Farmer.

Later, as we walked from the green, I overheard Zach the CEO saying, "Old Double Trouble kicked my butt today." He took off his hat and scratched his head. "It got me for a double bogey."

Matthew chimed in. "Maybe they should call it Double Trouble Double Bogey?" For good measure, the Parm delivered the message. He tacked on a thumbs up and a "Heeey."

If there was ever a time when Matthew should've kept his mouth shut, it was then. I wanted to explain how saying something like that could explode in his face. I paid dearly for not keeping my mouth shut. But wouldn't you know it. Matthew got away with it.

"Come here you," Mister Zach said, playfully grabbing Matthew around the neck and offering up a good-natured mussing of his hair. Mister Zach reached the cart and slid the putter back into the bag. He shook his head and announced to the crowd, "Old Double Trouble kicked my butt today." Whether he was looking for pity or some level of shared grief, he was showered with a few laughs. "On top of that, my caddy gives me a few kicks too." A few more chuckles flowed.

While I got glares and grumbles, Matthew collected a hug around the neck. Someday, I thought. Someday you won't be cute. Someday you'll lay an egg. The act will get stale. Your dreams will get stepped on.

But I tried to stay positive. That was one thing I had going for me. I didn't dwell too long on the negative. I started to think of something else. Like that nickname, Double Trouble.

Mister Zach referred to it like it was a person or foe. "Old Double Trouble kicked my butt today." I never understood that kind of thinking. Old Double Trouble doesn't fight back. It doesn't play defense. It doesn't prepare for you. It doesn't think. It had no personality. It's just a mountain that sits there waiting to be climbed. It's the difficult trail for a cross country runner or the white water foam of dangerous rapids for a kayaker. "Old Foamy Cascades kicked my butt today." The track or trail or challenge is not a living breathing foe out against someone. It's an obstacle. Everyone faces it. The course, the dreaded feature, is not what beats you; it's your competitor that performed better than you. It's you that beat you. I'd rather hear someone say, "I wasn't that good today." An inanimate object cannot claim victory over you. It cannot defeat you. It can only be used as an excuse. Yeah, I looked up inanimate. I guess even people trying to tell golf stories could use that excuse too. Like now. I think I'll say this old story is getting the best of me today. I think I'll just take a break. The words just weren't coming up right. The old IBM Selectric is kicking my butt today.

    Just kidding.

    Mister Zach and I had something in common. We shared some grief on the toughest hole on the golf course. On second thought, why not? Maybe I will blame that inanimate object. I didn't keep my mouth shut. I failed to follow that important caddy rule. Old Double Trouble kicked my butt too.

16

Roped-off spectators lined both sides of a path toward the next tee. A few hands were extended hoping for a high-five. I heard a woman's voice in the crowd. She was saying something like, "I think the President's a little ticked at his caddy." If those weren't the exact words, they were something like that. I'll give her credit for being such a keen observer. She must have been proud enough of her insight to share it with those around her. A real on-the-spot commentator. That grandstand crowd hoping to see the sparks and twisted metal crash of race cars would like to hear what she had to say. I didn't like the negative notoriety. Never mind the fact that she was probably right.

It made me think about the caddying job I had over the summer. I harbored similar feelings then. I quit after three weeks. It was probably because I was overly sensitive. I eventually shook off the negative feelings. I had gotten over it. Being asked to caddy for the President helped. It rekindled my dream of a caddying career. And even though it happened a few months before, it felt like ancient history. And no, this wasn't turning into a history story. There was no civil war. No rebellion. No revolution. No Washington crossing the Delaware. No Hannibal and his elephants. No Marco Polo. No Napoleon. It was Double

Trouble that had me thinking about my overly sensitive feelings. And the summer job was worth bringing up as a comparison.

There weren't enough lawns under my care to fund the car insurance premium. So, I decided to look for a job.

After seeing an ad in the local newspaper, I made a call. I was asked to show up on a Monday. I did it all on my own with no help from my mom. Better yet, I never mentioned my relation to Chuck Green. If the caddy master had known that I was his nephew, I'm sure he would've treated me differently. I would even bet that a few of the members would have treated me differently. But I never used his name. Again, I wanted to say I earned any success on my own. Either I was good enough, or I wasn't.

I figured being a caddy would be fun. I liked golf and being outdoors. I even had thoughts of someday making a career of it. The Monday I showed up was around Independence Day. The holiday brought out an army of golfers and the caddy reinforcements met the demand. The first week was a good one. It was new and exciting and the job came easy. The members didn't seem too discerning. Maybe it was due to a deep caddy pool. Or maybe the holiday put them in good spirits. But things changed in the two weeks that followed. Many members left town for summer vacations. Combined with a heat wave, the number of rounds played on the sweltering course dwindled. Those brave enough to battle the heat opted to ride in a cart. That alone was enough to send several halfhearted caddies packing.

Maybe it was the country club itself that initiated my overly sensitive feelings. It was an exclusive setting. Foundations, endowments, trust funds, a Rolls Royce with a driver. Grand Ballroom, men's grill, ladies' lounge. Pedigree. Old money, new money, estates with names, butlers, bidets, concierge. High walls and hedges. Fountains. Keep out the riff raff. A solarium. Power and privilege. Gates and gatekeepers. On my first day, I was pointed to a remote back entrance. Employees forbidden from the main entrance. And don't wander up near the clubhouse. When you're waiting for a bag, stay out in the yard with the rest of the caddies.

There were a string of days that I showed up and didn't get a bag. The country club at least paid a minimum fee for any caddy that showed up. It was barely enough for a hot dog and bus fare on the days my mom couldn't pick me up. Those days I saved nothing. I was at the bottom of the list. Whenever I did get a bag, it usually resulted in a minimum payout from a member that played golf twice a year. They were notoriously known as both poor golfers and even worst tippers. They rarely covered the eighteen holes in a straight line. You had to work twice as hard because it took them twice as many shots to get around. The regular caddies, the ones at the top of the list, knew to stay away from the 'twice-a-year' members. It didn't take me long to figure that out. And it didn't take long for me to figure out the nest egg for car insurance wasn't growing. That alone was reason enough to call it quits. But something else happened. I pulled the wrong pickup stick in KerPlunk and all the marbles came crashing down.

It happened on a day that I was saddled to the bag of the biggest bigwig at the country club. I thought such an assignment would give me a glimpse of how good it could be if only I got the right bag, if only I got the right member. But that wasn't the case.

Brandon M. Taylor III was known throughout the country club. He was the wealthiest, most powerful, and most outspoken member. He was an Icon of Industry, Business Baron, Wizard of Wall Street, and Tycoon. He inspected every blade of grass with exacting requirements giving the white glove treatment to everything. He nitpicked with a magnifying glass and often ranted about unacceptable levels of service. He rarely offered recognition for a job well done. Brandon M. Taylor III never smiled. He never joked. He never slapped a playing partner on the back. It made me think. If his time on the golf course was meant to be relaxing, enjoyable, leisurely, therapeutic, I would hate to see him when he was uptight. He had shown up late one afternoon and wanted to get in a round by himself before heading home for dinner. I was the only caddy left waiting in the yard.

At the end of the round, I handed over his golf bag to the guys working the bag room and they filed it away in storage. I didn't receive a tip. That was not so unusual, just disappointing. But that's not what discouraged me. As I walked back toward the caddy yard, I saw Brandon M. Taylor III speaking with the caddy master. I heard him saying, "Where you getting your caddies these days?" His hands were on his hips and he swiveled his head when he talked. I couldn't hear what he said next, but as he turned and started to walk away I heard him say, "You shouldn't let them out on the course until they know what they're doing."

Here was the funny thing. I couldn't tell you what I had done wrong. I had given it my best. If I had been lazy and not hustled, I could understand his gripe. I thought I had kept up. As I looked back on it, maybe it had something to do with not knowing enough to realize I wasn't doing a good job. I knew much more now. But like I said, I was trying.

I approached the caddy master. "Anything wrong?"

"Nah," he said. His head was down reviewing a list of tee times and caddy assignments for the next day. "Don't worry about it. He's just very meticulous. We'll talk about it later."

I felt lousy. And when I got home, I had to look up the word meticulous. It didn't make me feel any better.

Before falling asleep that night, negative voices swam around in my head. You shouldn't be a caddy. You're not cut out to be a caddy. You don't know what you're doing. You're carrying the bag all wrong. You know nothing about golf. You're not even good at golf. You're just toting a bag. You're falling behind. You're not supposed to be standing there. You're doing it all wrong. Others do it this way, why can't you? You're not following the rules. You're not keeping up. You're not doing what is expected. You don't seem to know what you're doing. You're boring. You're too excited. You're too quiet. You're too loud. You're not outgoing enough. You're too boastful. You're a real hack. You're doing it different. You're doing it the same. You don't fit in here. Good luck trying to fit in somewhere else. You'd be better off on a lawnmower or with a rake in your hands. You shouldn't even bother. People like you shouldn't even bother. Caddying is for others, not you. You don't stand a chance. You don't know the rules. You've never done this before. You're not prepared. You're not up to par. Everybody thinks they can be a caddy. Everybody thinks there's nothing to it. Is that what you think?

The voices in my head came from snobby country club members. I also heard Renee's voice. I heard the grounds crew.

There was also an old man down the street that doesn't even play golf. I heard old voices. I heard young voices. I even began to hear it from my own voice. The message didn't change.

I woke the next morning and called the caddy master. I told him my days of being a caddy at the country club were over.

When I heard the woman's voice in the crowd, "I think the President's a little ticked at his caddy," it brought me back to those doubtful voices. I couldn't help but feel the sting. But like my run-in with Brandon M. Taylor III, it didn't take long for me to get over it. At that point, most people would have given up. And if I said that I kept going and didn't give up on the thought of someday being a caddy for Uncle Charlie, most people would say that doesn't make sense. But like I've said before, my motivation didn't make much sense to me either. I knew one thing. I wasn't ready to give up. Especially since I was about to get a chance to talk with Major about that spiral notepad.

That chance came on the next hole. It was the second time during the day that the golf course layout allowed caddies to move ahead of the players on the tee. To show I had learned something, I had checked with the President before to make sure he had tees and an extra golf ball. I didn't come right out and ask him, but I had kept close enough eyes on him to notice his pockets were full. I also had learned to keep watch of the tee shots as they flew in our direction.

"Sure thing, Rook," said Major, pulling the notepad from his rear pocket. He flipped to a random page. "I keep notes on each course we play. Look here." He pointed. "I like to layout each hole and mark some yardages." There were diagrams of fairways and greens complete with bunkers and water hazards. There were shapes of putting greens with large and small arrows pointing downhill to indicate a slope. There were columns of numbers and symbols. "I like to jot down a few notes to remind me how each hole should play, what conditions to look for, and what areas to be aware of."

"It looks like a treasure map."

"I never thought about it that way, but I guess you're right." He handed me the spiral pad and I flipped through a few pages. I couldn't help but think that such information would make me a better caddy.

I wanted to learn more. "How long you been a caddy?"

"On tour fifteen years."

"Ever think about doing something else?"

"Me? Nah. My brother-in-law wanted me to work on his lot selling cars, but I turned him down. Told him maybe someday."

I decided to let him in on my career plans. "I'm thinking about being a caddy someday." I doubted he would give me the 'caddies are bums' speech.

"I think it's kind of a craft," Major said, scratching his chin. "The more you do it, the better you get. Come to think of it, I guess that's true about most things. But there really is no substitute for the long hours. And true, some people pick it up pretty quick and it comes easy. But it took me a long time. I've enjoyed the ride."

"I caddied some last summer."

"That's a good start," Major said. "To be a tour caddy, you have to love golf so much it's all you ever think about. The days are long and the prep work gets tedious. Most people think it's just four days of a tournament, but that's not true. Other days are spent on the range and practice rounds. The only time we get any rest is on the road. We basically eat and sleep golf. And when sleeping, we're usually dreaming about golf."

None of what he was saying deterred me. "You dream about golf?"

"I do," Major said. "And unfortunately you wouldn't believe how many nightmares are possible."

"Nightmares?"

"Never mind, Rook. You don't have to worry about nightmares."

It was funny how we had gotten onto the subject of dreams. It was almost like it was planned. "I do keep having this one dream."

"About golf?"

"No. About my teeth falling out."

"Your teeth?"

"Yeah. What do you think it means?"

"When was the last time you went to the dentist?"

We laughed and joked until the players arrived from the tee. I felt a real camaraderie with Major. I watched Chip Swanson on the other side of the fairway and felt equally good about the possibilities of someday matching him word for word with the flowery caddy advice.

The confidence I was feeling was fleeting.

It would only last until we made it to the putting green. There and then the Big Goof occurred.

17

I spotted Theresa Bellissima. She stood behind the ropes near the putting green. A slight breeze at her back blew her hair to the front of her face. She looked like a dream. As I walked next to the President, a smattering of applause followed us. He twirled his putter like a baton as he marched. His approach shot had found the fringe but was a lengthy distance from the hole. I split off to look for a convenient place to drop the bag. The idea was to position it so that once we completed the hole it would be en route to the next tee. The perfect resting place was right in front of Theresa Bellissima.

Mister Zach was still short of the green and had yet to chip on. And Ernie Banks was waiting to descend into a green-side bunker and blast out. I was hoping they would take their time.

When I laid the bag on the ground, Theresa Bellissima smiled. She was chewing gum. "You want a piece?" She held out the rectangular pack and slid out a flat stick wrapped in foil.

"Sure," I grabbed it, unwrapped it, stuffed it in my mouth, and started chewing. "Thunks." Sugary spearmint twisted my tongue and flooded my mouth with slobber. We were far enough away from the action to have a conversation albeit one that required hushed golf crowd voices. The whispering was something else we could share.

"You're so funny."

"Funny?" I didn't know what to say. Theresa Bellissima looked puzzled too. "You wanna hear something funny?" I fumbled around looking for something. "You ever have a funny dream?"

She brushed the hair from her face. "A funny dream?"

"Yeah," I said, quickly realizing that I could tell her I was dreaming about her. But I wasn't that bold. "Like you had lost a tooth or something." Maybe I wanted to show her my sensitive side. Maybe she knew what it meant.

She looked confused. "A tooth?"

"Awe, forget it."

She smiled. "You're so funny."

I guess there wasn't much of a joke there. "Just kidding." I laughed and played along. "I saw this caddy today that was missing his front teeth."

That's when she surprised me. "I want to ask you something." She flashed a coy smile.

Ernie Banks climbed out of the bunker and struck at the upturned sole of his golf shoe. A layer of caked on sand dropped to the earth. It wasn't much of a stretch to picture him going through the same routine outside the batter's box with a wooden bat handle striking at metal cleats.

"I gotta go," I said, trotting up a slope to the green. The clock was striking midnight. I turned and said, "Talk to you later."

She smiled and waved.

The President was crouched on the fringe surveying the slope of the green. He handed me his golf ball and I wiped it clean with the towel draped over my neck. I started thinking about Theresa Bellissima. What was she going to ask me? Was it about Algebra? Was she going to ask for my phone number? Maybe she wanted me to ask for her phone number. There was a Sadie Hawkins dance at our school in the fall when girls asked guys to a dance. Was she going to ask me to the Sadie Hawkins dance? It had to be something good like that.

"Son," I heard the President say. It took me a couple of seconds to realize he was talking to me. It would have helped if he had looked in my direction when he said it. "Will you get the pin?"

"Um, yessir." Having noticed none of the other caddies around, I hustled toward the flagstick.

All day I had waited for the opportunity. I had been relegated to bystander on previous occasions as Major and Chip Swanson took turns standing like soldiers holding the flagstick. As putts rolled toward them, they lifted the pin from the cup. I figured that tending the flag was the ultimate in caddydom. And now, it was my turn on center stage. All eyes would focus on me as the ball rolled toward the target. Even the President would focus his aim in my direction. He would depend on me to carry out a real caddying duty. It was a pinnacle. He finally saw me open and was throwing me the ball. All I had to do was watch where I stood and pull the flag from the cup at the right time. How simple it all sounded.

Now there were a number of things I could have blamed for what happened next, starting first with my growing exhaustion. My shoulders grew sore. My legs were getting weak. My arms sagged. I was certainly tired and thirsty when the Big Goof occurred and nothing good usually happens when you're tired and thirsty. And although I haven't come right out and said it, I felt some pressure being the caddy for the President. I began to feel the weight of being on high alert for well over three and a half hours, in front of the cameras with large lenses, the Secret Service agents with their hidden walkie-talkies, and the hordes of onlookers. I was shooting for extraordinary for the President, for Uncle Charlie, for myself. I had expended blood, sweat and tears. Maybe the pressure of all that responsibility wore me down to a breaking point. There was also Teresa Bellissima. Catching a glimpse of her at exactly the wrong time certainly was a distraction.

All the excuses sounded reasonable, but there was no escaping the truth. I was the only person that could be blamed for the Big Goof. It was me that got complacent. It was only me standing out there on center stage. Everyone saw that it was me that disrupted the tournament. It was my fault. I fumbled.

I stood holding the pin. The President looked over his lengthy putt. The flag fluttered above my head. I felt a growing confidence. I was a conqueror claiming a plot of the new world. I was planting Old Glory on the moon. I was on top of a mountain, having reached the peak after an excruciating climb, and ready to plant the marker into the frozen earth. I remembered how both Major and Chip Swanson reached high grabbing the flag and pinning it tight against the pole to keep its movement from being a distraction. I reached high and did the same.

I couldn't resist sneaking a glance toward Theresa Bellissima. I was feeling stronger, larger, and more capable. She could see me there holding the flag and realize I could provide for her. She should be thinking about how I was big enough, strong enough, and smart enough to give her whatever she wanted for the rest of her life. I was a good catch. My jaws worked on the gum. I wanted Theresa Bellissima. I wanted to escape with her. So, in my mind, we were together. We were together on a deserted island...the sun glistening on her oily tan as she lounged in a lime-green string bikini. A gentle breeze roused waves of ocean that lapped into shallow pools in the shifting sand. Her puckered glossy lips drew on a straw extending from a coconut. She asked me, What're you thinking? I took a deep breath and shrugged without a care. Oh, nothing. Sure. Carefree. Just the two of us. No one else in the entire world existed. I reached up and touched my chin. No pimples there. What are you doing? She would say. Oh, nothing. She would glance above her sunglasses and say, You're so handsome. I could snap my fingers and anything I wanted would appear. A cold drink. A pair of sunglasses. A paper umbrella for my own coconut drink. But I already had everything that I wanted; I was staring at Theresa Bellissima in a string bikini. She laughed at my jokes and clung to every word.

From fifty feet away, the President finally made the putting stroke that started the ball across the immaculate green. As it climbed over a mound and headed for the cup, I realized it was my cue to lift the flagstick from the hole. With the grip that steadied the flag in the breeze, I tried to lift. Nothing moved. Maybe, I thought, since I had such a high grip, I was already extended as high as I could reach and that's why there was no movement. I let loose of the flag and grabbed the center of the stick. I tugged. Nothing moved. The pin was frozen in place. It was all happening too fast. The golf ball was closing in. I began to panic. I grabbed the pin with both hands and pulled. Again, it didn't budge. What was happening? There was no time to think. I bent my knees and tried to draw it out using the strength of my legs. A fruitless squire attempting to pull Excalibur from the stone. The ball was closing in with plenty of speed. I lifted with my legs. I felt the flagstick give. As I drew the pin higher, it felt heavier than it should. The rolling golf ball was two feet away. I looked down and noticed a metal cylinder protruding from the earth. It was the entire metal cup. It was a spectacle no less subtle than a misguided backhoe operator wandering onto the green, and with the diesel engine roaring, ripping into the sod with its clawed bucket and hoisting a buried cast iron drainpipe. The President's golf ball, with plenty of speed and on a perfect line, crashed into the side of the raised metal housing. As the ball bounced off the exposed vertical pipe, a dull clang resonated like a rubber stopper on a wind chime. I heard gasps from the crowd. I saw the amazed look on the President's face. I felt the blood draining from my limbs. I stood there on the world's stage holding a flagstick fused to the metal cup that had been raised above the putting surface. Complete humiliation. The Big Goof.

After crashing into the exposed obstacle, the golf ball continued rolling. I thought about those race cars at the speedway smashing into the metal guard rails. I looked toward the President. The man a whole nation depended upon in a crisis to remain calm, cool, and collected appeared to be shocked and bewildered. Both of my hands remained on the flexing flagstick with the chunk of metal at the bottom. There was no place to hide. There was no one else to blame. All caddy rules had been obliterated. I wanted to return to that beach with Theresa Bellissima. Gasps and murmurs from the roped gallery had drowned out the wishful crashing of waves. My dreams of someday being a caddy on the professional tour were washed out to sea.

Major grabbed the flagstick from me and stuffed the canister back in the ground. It was as if he had lowered a periscope on the sea of green. With an iron club in his hand he hammered at the base of the pin in hopes that it would loosen itself. When that didn't work, he stepped on the rim of the cup with both feet and lifted. With a little extra effort the cup released its grip and the stick came free. The metal housing remained in the ground. There was a smattering of applause from the crowd.

I was in a fog. I surrendered whatever remaining flagstick responsibilities to Major and drifted toward the shadows on the edge of the green. "Hey Bionic Man," Chip Swanson whispered. "I didn't realize you were that strong. You must pump a lot of iron." He ended the ribbing with a footnote. "It's good to check first to make sure the pin will come out."

Another caddy rule that I had failed to follow. "No one told me that," I whispered, ashamed and defensive. The more I thought about it, a good caddy wouldn't have to be told such things. A good caddy would've paid close enough attention to pick up on this rule. I wasn't going to admit that to Chip Swanson, but I knew there were no excuses.

The Big Goof was like getting pushed off a cliff. My confidence took a nosedive. I was tumbling into an abyss. And I guess it really wasn't like getting pushed off a cliff, it was more like waltzing over the edge without realizing the danger.

Show up, keep up, and keep your mouth shut. If it were up to me, I'd add one more. Don't throw up. Because that's what I felt like doing; losing my lunch right then and there. Barf-o-rama. Pukefest. A regal regurgitation. Blow chunks. Hoo-hash.

The caddy rules were supposed to be simple and easy to follow. Maybe they should be rewritten to include an even lower threshold for the really idiotic. They may even call it the Sam Parma Rule. It would read something like: Under no circumstance, nor on any occasion, whether on purpose, by accident or incompetence, should a caddy interfere, halt, impede, divert, intercept, or by any other means, the assigned player's (or anyone in the same group, or for that matter, anyone on or off the golf course) attempt, turn, play, traveling golf ball, and or insert any action effecting the outcome of any single stroke, for the entirety of the time assigned the golf bag. (For you real dummies, here's an example: When standing on the green (smooth putting surface) tending the flag (holding the flagstick in the cup because the person aiming at the hole is too far away to see it) or performing other duties (or plain loitering), always pay attention (do not daydream or get distracted – especially if hot babes are around) and first check to see if the flagstick is not stuck in the hole so that if any putts (chip shots, bunker shots or any other advancements towards the hole) coming from your player (or any other in the group for that matter) start rolling in your direction, you have maintained enough interest in your work, and have the concentration level of a baboon, to lift the flagstick from the hole without unearthing the underground golf course infrastructure. Also, if you happen to be standing, kneeling, and otherwise in the path of the oncoming rolling, bouncing, skittering golf ball, for God's sake, please move out of the way. Violating this rule in front of large crowds or while caddying for national dignitaries such as the President of the United States will certainly result in humiliation, shame, disdain, and will produce an opportunity for ridicule from every person over the age of two.

Penalties for such infractions include sheer and utter disdain from the person you are caddying for because they will incur a two-stroke penalty or loss of hole in match play. The offending caddy shall suffer total embarrassment, humiliation, and be ostracized by the golfing community for a period of no less than ten years. Should you ever attempt to break into the professional tour as a caddy, violations of the Sam Parma Rule will remain on your permanent record and will definitely be taken into consideration. Questions should be raised by a committee as to whom the responsible parties for ever letting such a numbskull caddy on the golf course in the first place.

I heard the President's voice, "What's the rule on that Chuck?"

Major held the flagstick now. My mind went blank. I'm not sure what happened next. I wasn't even sure if the President continued on the green or went back and replayed his shot.

I thought about the President. I had given him enough material to banter with playing partners for the next thirty years. I'm sure he'll bring it up the next time he's in Singapore, playing with the President of Singapore. I'm sure he'll do the same in Ireland, Australia, and India. And no, I didn't bother to look up the fact if Singapore has a president, a king, or a dictator. It doesn't matter. I think you get the point.

The thought of providing extraordinary service was blown to bits. Well, I guess in some way, the Big Goof was out-of-the-ordinary. I could hear the story now that the President would be telling those foreign dignitaries and celebrities on golf courses around the world. "I once had this caddy at the Capital City Pro-Celebrity," he would say. "And what he did was quite out of the ordinary." Note the meaning of extraordinary had moved into the negative light. The service level I provided ranked among the strange, bizarre, and wacky.

18

Not much happened on the last two holes. All I could remember was having a numb feeling all over. Once I surrendered the flagstick to Major, it was like I was walking around in a daze. The sun was lower in the sky and everything looked smoky. As we climbed the eighteenth fairway, I realized the round was coming to a conclusion. But in reality, things came to an end for me two holes before. Goodnight John Boy.

Before we finished, I think Chip Swanson called me the Bionic Man a few more times. And I'm almost sure Ernie Banks patted me on the back and smiled. He probably said something nice as well, but I couldn't remember enough of it to repeat. He was about the nicest celebrity I ever met. Major probably gave me one or two other final tips on being a good caddy. Not that I wanted to relive the Big Goof anymore, but I'm sure one of the tips had to do with the flagstick. I think he said something like, "Pull it out when you first take hold and lean it in the hole." I wasn't really listening. At that point, I was almost certain that I was going to give up any thoughts of ever being a caddy.

Mister Zach was the last player to sink a putt on the eighteenth green. After that, caps were removed and handshakes and smiles were swapped. The round was over. It was the end of the line. The traveling throng that had followed us from the beginning began to disperse. Spectators in the grandstands funneled to the aisles and down the narrow steps. I remained near the President. He remained behind the ropes while making his way to a large scoreboard. Matthew inched the cart through the crowd. Mister Zach remained in the passenger's seat smiling and waving. A Secret Service agent approached me. "I'll take it from here, kid," he said. I eased the bag from my shoulder. And just like that, the pressing weight of the day was lifted. The burden was gone. I felt lighter. I watched the agent slide away with the bag and thought about all the compartments that I never had to chance to search through. The way the bag was whisked away allowed my suspicions to grow. It was possible I had in my possession something vital. If the time was right the next day, maybe I would sneak a peek.

But the more I thought about it, I started to dread another day like the one I had. The experience had left me full of doubt. My confidence was drained.

And then, an idea came to me. Maybe Chip Swanson should carry the President's bag the next day. He was clearly a better caddy. And the President deserved to have the best. Somehow, if I got the chance, I would bring the idea to Uncle Charlie. He would know how to handle it. And better yet, if Chip Swanson was to caddy for the President, maybe I could then carry the bag for Ernie Banks. It certainly seemed like a fair swap. It would make my job easier. Maybe even fun.

I felt a slap on the back, "See you around, Steve Austin." It was Chip Swanson.

"Yeah," I nodded. "See you around." At least he continued to acknowledge my existence.

The President stood talking to Uncle Charlie. He looked in my direction and started patting his pockets. "How much do I owe you, young man?"

I looked over to Uncle Charlie. His eyebrows were raised.

I knew this was a delicate situation. I smiled. "Nothing, sir."

Uncle Charlie smiled.

"Well," the President said, looking around for possible assistance. "It looks like I don't have my wallet on me."

"That's okay, sir." I said, nodding and smiling.

The President looked again over to Uncle Charlie, then to me. "You're going to be my caddy tomorrow?"

"Yessir." I thought about bringing up the idea to swap caddies, but quickly figured it wasn't the right time.

He patted again at his pockets. "I'll be sure to take care of you then." He smiled then slapped Uncle Charlie on the back. "See you inside?"

"Yes sir." Uncle Charlie nodded and smiled.

I wanted to make the point that I wasn't doing the job for the money, but decided to keep my mouth shut.

A different Secret Service agent lifted the rope and escorted the President, along with a few local cops, toward the clubhouse. They didn't stop until they got inside the glass double doors.

Uncle Charlie lingered awhile signing a few autographs. I just stood around trying to figure out what to do next. He looked over to me. "You're all set?"

"Sure," I nodded. "Mom'll be here soon."

Uncle Charlie continued signing autographs. "You need a ride in the morning?"

"She's bringing us."

"See you then?" He started walking and signing at the same time.

"Yep." I gave him a halfhearted wave. "Thanks."

I was still in that fog and in no hurry. I stood beneath the giant scoreboard and looked around. I watched as the crowds, sunburned and sweaty, herded through the exits. Turnstiles had been removed and the army of ticket checkers dismissed. A pile of litter surrounded a garbage can that was filled past capacity. A few players loitered on the practice tee hoping to find areas for improvement before the next round. The cart barn doors were swung open. Inside, the heavy equipment was absent. Crews were out replenishing the fairways and roughs that were trampled from the stampede. On the first fairway, the irrigation system sprung to life. The spray was beating around in circles.

Matthew came strolling past. "Come and get me when Mom gets here," he said, flashing a grin. With pinched fingers, he held both ends of a twenty dollar bill. He began yanking it to make a snapping noise. "I'm going for ice cream." He never slowed down.

I didn't know if he was rubbing in the fact that my pockets were empty. Or if he thought I had been paid the same and he was proving that we were on the same level. Matthew generally thought about himself first. So I doubted if he even cared that I had nothing to show for the day of work.

I untied the strings on both sides of the vest and lifted it over my head. The red blood stain across the logo had turned brown. I approached one of the tournament officials beneath the giant scoreboard. I held up the caddy vest now rolled up in my hand. "We suppose to turn this in somewhere?"

He looked around. "You working tomorrow?"

I hesitated. "Yeah." I hoped he wouldn't hold me to my word. I wasn't exactly sure if I would return for another round of humiliation.

"Then hang onto it."

"Okay."

I peeled the visor from my head. A white jagged line, a salt streak, marked a peak on the dark green felt under the bill. The sweat had begun to recede towards the headband. I unpinned the badge that read, CADDY. I didn't feel worthy of the rank. I was an imposter. I stuffed the button in my pocket.

That's when I spotted Theresa Bellissima. She was smiling and sashaying in my direction. I wondered if she was a witness to the Big Goof. She had to be. She was part of the distraction.

"You were hilarious," she said, almost breaking out in laughter. "I didn't know you were so funny."

"Funny?"

"You had the whole crowd going."

"Really?"

"Yeah," she nodded and smiled. She acted like it was a foregone conclusion that I was the next Nipsey Russell.

I didn't think she realized the humiliation. Seeing her smiling at me started to chase away the numb feelings. She could make anyone feel better. She could lift me from the doldrums. I was down, but not out. I thought about what she last said. "Earlier," I stammered. "You said you wanted to ask me something?" I had nothing to lose. No more beating around the bush. All her subtle hints were leading up to this moment. Was she going to ask me to the Sadie Hawkins dance?

She started twisting her hair around a finger. She glanced toward the ground and started running the toe-end of her sandal through the grass. "Isn't that Chip Swanson over there?" She pointed.

"Yeah," I said.

"Do you know if he has a girlfriend?"

It took all my strength to keep my face from falling. "I don't know. I just met him."

"Well," she said. "Will you tell him I think he's cute?"

And that was that. A stab, directly in the heart. How dumb could I be? I should've known I wasn't on the same level as Chip Swanson. I should've known I wasn't in Theresa Bellissima's league. How did I get the signals so messed up? I never really had a chance with her.

"You should tell him yourself." I spit out while trying to muster a smile.

"Oh, I couldn't do that."

That's when I thought about playing hardball. I had heard the saying that all was fair in love and war. I thought about telling her that Chip Swanson wasn't all that wonderful. I thought about telling her that he was afraid of snakes. It was his kryptonite. If I brought him down a peg, maybe should would look at me differently. Maybe I would have a chance. But I wasn't that kind of guy.

"Maybe tomorrow," I said. "If I get a chance."

"Would you? Oh, that would be so sweet." She smiled. "See you tomorrow."

"Yeah." She had no idea that I was thinking of never showing my face around there again.

I wondered if the Big Goof had cost me any chance with Theresa Bellissima. I was sure no one would ever ask such and idiot to the Sadie Hawkins dance. The Sam Parma Rule. She would be embarrassed to be seen anywhere with me. Much less go out on a date. Or, was she interested in Chip Swanson from the very beginning? Had I misread her intentions in the first place? I felt the stabbing pain because I thought I had lost her. But after thinking about it, I guess I couldn't really loose something I never had in the first place. I had been chewing the spearmint gum she had given me. It began to taste bitter. I found a trash can and spit it out. I started for the parking lot.

A groundskeeper on the tenth tee was filling divots with green sand from a scoop and bucket. A pile of ice dumped from the coolers melted in the grass. Ahead of him, another worker tugged a hose across the green and began watering the fringe. The flagstick had been removed. Gas engines on blowers, strapped to workers like backpacks, roared in the emptied grandstand. Clouds of dust and debris blanketed them. It reminded me of Pigpen. I looked around for Renee and spotted her under a tree talking to some dopey-looking dude.

"We're sposed to be waiting in the parking lot," I said.

"I know. I'm watching."

"You can't see the parking lot from here."

"Yes I can. I've been watching for twenty minutes."

I looked over the older dude she was talking to. He had on a dopey shirt, dopey pants, and dopey shoes. His eyes looked dopey. Maybe it was the dopey moustache that made him look older. "Who's this?" I couldn't pinpoint what it was about him I didn't like. Maybe it was that he was dopey.

"None of your business," she snarled and turned her back to me. "I can see from here."

I wasn't in the mood for an argument. I turned and walked away. Maybe the thing I didn't like about Mister Moustache was the fact that he was wearing the visor that Uncle Charlie had given Renee. Then again, maybe I didn't like Renee for giving it to him.

I passed behind a corporate tent. A chorus of laughter and cheers from a live band seeped through the canvas walls. Beats from a bass drum pounded my brain. It wasn't much of a stretch to imagine Matthew on the other side in the midst of the partying crowd. He was probably doing the Birdie Dance on top of a table. In one hand he was probably holding a frosty milkshake and in the other a tip jar. He would be shimmying and grinning. The Parm was giving the crowd one last thumbs up.

I reached the parking lot and took a seat on the curb. I placed the rolled-up caddy bib on the ground next to me. While waiting for my ride home, I propped my elbows on my thighs and started tossing pebbles. An ant scurried across the pavement.

19

And there you have it. Now you know how I arrived at the low spot. Now you know how the day had gone and all the reasons why I was feeling futile. With my head lowered and the rolled up bib on the ground next to me, I started tossing pebbles. But before I get to what happened next, I should explain why it was so important.

Now that I looked back on it, I know that what happened next was more than just a stroking of my ego. At least that's what I hoped. What I mean to say is I don't think it fueled my vanity on any level. I was the teen with pimples on his chin. And I had reminded myself the only reason I had gotten the caddy job in the first place was my good fortune of being related to Uncle Charlie. And he set a pretty good example of someone not getting an inflated ego.

And I don't want to make a big fuss over what happened next, except for the fact that there probably wouldn't be much of a story without it. Simple as it was, there was no changing the fact that it left me feeling good and lifted me from the doldrums. It made the whole day feel worthwhile. I knew the ending was important. I wouldn't even start telling the story before I knew how it ended.

Maybe what made it important were all the discoveries I had made during the day. How much I missed certain winks and nods of approval. What it really meant to be rewarded for a job well done. What it meant to try to be extraordinary. What it means to follow rules and guidelines. How to take criticism. How much I wanted to be a caddy. What I could learn from watching others that were good at being caddies. What it means to be lucky, popular, or good. All these things came to me. But they wouldn't have been so evident if what happened next had not occurred. Maybe that's why I said it seemed so simple, yet it meant so much.

After what happened next, I came away with a new feeling. A self-satisfaction. I realized there was a reward for all the hard work. A level of confidence came back. I was ready for the next day. I was ready to try again.

I've heard the saying that it is better to have loved and lost than to have never loved at all. And I bet you're thinking I'm going to say something about Theresa Bellissima. But, I'm not. I am thinking more of a general application that has to do with winners and losers. Most people would label the loser as the defeated one at the end of a contest. But I thought about how the loser was the one that decided to never enter the competition. The loser is the one cowering on the sidelines afraid to enter the game. I decided that it was better to have fought and lost than to have never fought at all. I thought about the time I played in my first junior golf tournament. I was in the battle. I had even shed some blood to prove it. What happened next wasn't necessarily a nod for a job well done. To me, it was a reminder. It was recognition. It was a realization that I had tried. I gave it my best, and someone had noticed the effort.

Like I said already, I was feeling futile sitting on the curb waiting for my ride home. Matthew was inside the corporate tent drowning himself with milkshakes and encore performances of the Birdie Dance. He suffered the day being showered with gifts.

My mind was a stew of doubts. I was ready to give up the idea of ever being a caddy. I was thinking that I should've paid more attention to the Caddy Master's speech that first day at the country club. I should've tried to be a lifeguard. When Uncle

Charlie first asked me to caddy for the President, I should've politely changed the subject and asked if he new any country club swimming pool managers. But what happened next made it all worthwhile. I realized that making it to the ranks of a professional tour caddy wasn't all that important. What happened next was enough of a reward and sufficient recognition that even if my stint as a caddy was short, it meant something.

I wondered if I had blown the opportunity of a lifetime. Not many people got a chance to caddy for the President of the United States. Initially I thought the opportunity meant I would be making a lifelong friend. If I ever got in a jam, I could ring up my old pal the President and he could bail me out. The big dose of reality that came on Saturday dashed those thoughts. After the Big Goof, he probably thought so little of me that he wouldn't even call me Farmer. My less-than-extraordinary performance had me feeling more likely to be deserving of the witness protection program. The Secret Service agents will probably remember me. I'd even bet there would be a footnote in their future clearance reports for me as a possible threat to national security.

And Theresa Bellissima. I was such a fool. I put myself out there and found the going rough. Was it her that approached as I sat there? Did she have second thoughts and start declaring an undying love for me? Is that the thing that would lift me from the curb? Anyone expecting a romantic scenario like that will be disappointed. This was no love story. No Princess and the Pauper. No Beauty and the Beast. I was no Lance Romance. I grabbed another pebble and tossed it in the air.

But what did happen next dissolved all the negative thoughts swimming around in my head. Afterwards, I wondered how I could've ever thought about giving up. What happened next gave me confidence. It changed my mind about Chip Swanson taking over my duties the next day. I would not surrender. The new attitude had me looking forward to Sunday. What happened next gave me a boost. The sun would come out on Sunday. It was the lift I needed.

"Excuse me mister." I heard a young voice. I looked up and saw the outline of a young boy and girl. The sun behind them

gave them a bright aura. They couldn't have been more than eight
or nine years old. The boy actually addressed me as mister.

I was still grabbing and tossing pebbles as if they were
dice. "Who, me?"

"Sure," he said. "I hope we're not bothering you." Sweat
trailed down his reddened cheek. A cardboard Bumble Bee Bakery
ticket tied to his belt loop fluttered in the breeze. He was clutching
a white golf hat in one hand and a ballpoint in the other. The hat
was covered with signatures.

"You're not bothering me," I said, stretching my legs to
stand. "And you shouldn't bother calling me mister." I thought
about Ernie Banks. "The only mister I know," I said, "is my dad."

The boy smiled, but I'm not sure he got the joke. He held
up the blazing white golf cap. "Will you sign?"

I was puzzled. "Sign your hat?"

"Please sir."

"Um—" I was more than a little confused. He had to know
I hadn't played in the tournament. My own sweaty visor and shirt
had to be enough so that he hadn't confused me with any teenage
movie star or pop singer. There were no limo chauffeurs, no
photographers, and no other autograph seekers within a thousand
feet. I was just some kid sitting on the curb waiting for his ride
home. "Um—I guess so."

He handed me the hat. I pointed to one of the signatures,
"Hey, you got one from Ernie Banks." I was reluctant to mess up
the hat with my name.

"Yessir." The kid flashed a huge grin.

"That's pretty cool," I said.

"Thank you, sir."

He handed me the ink pen. I looked around almost feeling
silly. I had the brand new hat in one hand and the pen in the other.
Maybe someone was playing a practical joke. Any minute I was
expecting Matthew to come charging out from behind a hedge
howling with laughter and pointing his finger at me.

But that didn't' happen.

I looked back down at the kid. "You sure you want me to
sign?"

He smiled and nodded. "Please."

Not wanting to be left out, the young girl raised her program. "It's nice to meet you."

"Nice to meet you too." I couldn't help but return the smile. I now held the program and cap in the same hand. It was full of all the treasured signatures they had collected.

I looked around again.

Beyond the fence behind the tenth green was a motorcycle cop in helmet, sunglasses, and gloves. His pants were tucked into his leather boots. He was parked in the middle of the street blowing whistle spurts and waving a stiff arm at a line of slow-moving traffic.

I thought about Renee. Maybe she had devised the practical joke. She was probably lurking behind the cart barn watching as the thing unfolded. Mister Moustache was probably in on it too. They both had probably paid off these kids. She probably had her camera waiting in front of her face with a finger poised over the button, just waiting for me to go for the bait. I stood there hooked with the pen, cap, and program. All she had to do was reel me in. It was a chance to catch me looking goofy in full-color-spectrum, pan-a-vision, zoom-lens fashion.

But the minutes unfolded. There were no trap doors. No surprises sprung. No laughing riot. "You got some good ones here." I was again hesitant because it appeared they had both done a nice job gathering a pretty impressive array of autographs. I didn't want to ruin the collection by adding my name. Maybe they didn't know the difference between somebody famous and just a regular schlep like me. When no one rushed from hiding, I decided maybe both the kids were just confusing me with someone else. "You're sure you want me to sign?"

"Yes, please." Whether they had confused me with someone else or even if this was some kind of joke, I couldn't go on without honoring the request. I found some space on the bill right next to Ernie Banks' autograph and signed my name in small letters, *Sam Parma*. Not *Sam Farmer*. Not *Sam Green*. Not *The Parm*. Not *Steve Austin*. Just plain old *Sam Parma*.

As I handed it back, the kid stared at my signature. "Thanks mister," he said with a big smile.

I half-expected him to look at my name and realize its insignificance. I assumed he would get upset that I had wrecked his perfectly good souvenir with my scribbled name. But that didn't happen either.

I wrote my name on the girl's program.

She smiled just as big and thanked me.

I just shrugged.

As they walked away, I remained standing. I was still puzzled. But I did feel a little taller.

I watched the kids as they ran in the direction of two waiting adults. I was curious. It wasn't much of a stretch to assume it was their mom and dad. As they rushed into their waiting arms I watched both parents smile and nod. The father draped an arm over the boy's shoulders. Bumble Bee Bakery tickets fluttered from all their belt loops. I would bet the day was their first time to ever be on the grounds of the country club. They huddled together to observe the latest adornment. "Did you get it?" I heard the mother say.

Both kids nodded and smiled.

"Tell me again," I then heard the father say to his son. "Who was that?"

I was expecting the father to start laughing. He would lightheartedly joke with them about getting an autograph from the wrong person. He would set them straight. He would explain that the new signature on the cap and program is bogus. You made a mistake. That person over there is a nobody.

But he didn't.

Instead, both kids looked up. They remained in a cheerful mood. They both looked at the autograph. The girl even ran a finger over it. They were almost insulted that the father had questioned their judgment. They both maintained an air that everyone on the golf course would've known whom the newly-acquired autograph came from. It was obvious to both the boy and girl. The boy pointed over to me. He nodded, smiled, and said, "That's the President's caddy."

CPSIA information can be obtained at www.ICGtesting.com
Printed in the USA
BVOW05s1744040614

355387BV00002B/121/P